Patricia Aird

THE HAWK AND
THE EAGLE

Limited Special Edition. No. 3 of 25 Paperbacks

The author took part in a training dig in Norfolk before going on to study archaeology and classics at Bristol University. After taking a master's degree at Sheffield, she worked all over the country on rescue excavations and went on to specialise in Roman pottery research.

She has worked for Historic England and has co-authored a number of research articles. She is widowed with two children and now lives in Hampshire.

To Jo and Sam

Patricia Aird

THE HAWK AND THE EAGLE

AUSTIN MACAULEY PUBLISHERS™

LONDON • CAMBRIDGE • NEW YORK • SHARJAH

A CIP catalogue record for this title is available from the British Library.

ISBN 9781528940634 (Paperback)
ISBN 9781528970419 (ePub e-book)

www.austinmacauley.com

First Published (2020)
Austin Macauley Publishers Ltd
25 Canada Square
Canary Wharf
London
E14 5LQ

Although *The Hawk and the Eagle* is a novel, many of the historic events detailed relating to the Boudiccan rebellion did actually happen and have been chronicled by Tacitus in his Annals, Histories and Life of Agricola which are available to read on the internet.

Thanks to the Internet Classics Archive. I am indebted to the scholarship of Graham Webster (in *Rome Against Caratacus: The Roman Campaigns in Britain AD 48-58* published by Book Club Associates London 1981) and Sheppard Frere (in *Britannia: A History of Roman Britain* published by Routeledge and Kegan Paul in 1978) for their analysis of the archaeology and historic sources which made it possible to imagine other events which may have happened at that time. The story of Gwenneth and Marcus is my own invention but illustrates what might have happened when Roman soldiers started to settle in the new province of Britannia. My own excavation experience has informed the technical details of life on a dig but the dig itself is entirely imaginary as are the characters taking part.

Chapter 1

In the year when Caesennius Paetus and Petronius Turpilianus were appointed to the consulate there was severe trouble in Britain.

Tacitus Annals 14.29.1

'We must make the living sacrifice.' The druid's words rang out in the silence, but there was a faint tremor in his voice.

The queen continued to wipe the spittle that dribbled down the chin of the man lying unconscious on the bed as if the druid had not spoken. 'Prepare more of your medicine.'

The druid stared at her back.

'Now,' she commanded.

The druid crouched down again by the fire and took a leather pouch from the bag that hung from the rope around his waist. With a deft movement, he shook fine powder into his left hand. Curling his nails into his palm, he thrust his fist into the flames. The acrid smell of burning flesh cut through the sweet odour of the sickroom as a thin stream of yellow oozed between his fingers and dripped into the rust-red liquid bubbling in the pot on the hearth. He poured a little of the potion into a hollowed-out horn.

'The medicine is ready.'

The queen turned to take the horn noting the blistered skin on his hand. At the height of his power, the skin would have been unblemished by the fire. His medicine was useless. She ignored the horn he held out to her and turned back to look at her husband on the bed. His face was pale in the glow of the firelight. His bloodless lips were stretched wide in a lopsided grimace and saliva trickled in a thin stream from one corner of his mouth. A rattle punctuated each laboured breath. She turned back to look at the druid.

'My husband is dying.'

'That is why we need the sacrifice.'

'No, the Romans have spies everywhere. We must not give them the excuse they want to claim our kingdom.'

'They will take it anyway if your husband dies.'

'There is still a chance. Gwenneth will find her brother. Then we will have the male heir we need to stop the Romans seizing our land and taking away our power.'

'She will fail. I have seen it in the runes.'

The queen sprang to her feet. 'How dare you seek to know the future without my consent?'

In two strides, she reached the druid crouching by the hearth. He cowered in anticipation of the blow threatened by her raised hand, but it didn't come. A low moan had drawn her back to her husband's bedside. She took a cloth from the bowl of water at her feet and wiped the sweat from his forehead. Then she turned back to the druid.

'So, the kingdom will be lost.'

The druid sensed an opportunity.

'Let me try the sacrifice,' he wheedled.

The queen looked at the floor, her brows drawn together in a frown. She did not need the runes to confirm what she already suspected. Her niece Gwenneth was just as uninterested in the kingdom as Corin her brother. Even if they found each other, it was doubtful either would return. The pair of them were loyal to their father's tribe, not her own. She railed inwardly at her own inability to produce a son, just two spineless daughters. If they hadn't needed a male heir, she would never have fostered the two brats after her their parents died. It had been a relief when Corin ran away as soon as he reached adolescence.

The queen dragged her thoughts back to the present. The druid's powers were waning, but maybe he had magic enough to keep her husband alive a few more days, time enough for her to find a way to preserve the kingdom. He still had influence over some of the elders so she needed to keep the druid on her side for now and, after all, what harm could it do to perform the sacrifice? The Romans knew very little of their rituals, and she had, so far, managed to keep her husband's illness a secret.

'Go, then,' she said at last. 'Find your victim. But make sure there is nothing that traces it back to us.'

'Have no fear. My searchers are well-trained.'

He uncurled his scrawny limbs from the squatting position he had assumed by the fire, gathered up the instruments and materials of his trade and stuffed them into his bag, to take advantage of the sudden weakness of his queen. The woven drapes swung back behind him as he passed into the deserted hall.

***

Gerry wrinkled her nose. The waiting room at Colchester bus station was enclosed on three sides with scratched Perspex screens, and she guessed it had been used as an alternative to the alleyway at the back when the nearby gents was closed at night. The bright orange plastic chairs were bolted to the concrete floor and each other, but why anyone would want to make off with them was a mystery, she thought. The bum-shaped depression that was supposed to be a seat had clearly been moulded from a size nought model and she could only perch on the edge, although she was slim by anyone's standards and now had pins and needles in her legs where the plastic cut into the top of her thighs.

She had exhausted all the possibilities her phone offered to relieve the tedium of waiting. She had even taken a selfie, although, unlike most of her friends, she was not in the habit of regularly changing her social media image. The face looking up at her from the screen had a stern expression and the usual smile was absent. The tan she had acquired on her travels, despite her fair skin, enhanced the green of her eyes, she thought; and the pixie cut to her copper hair was a good choice – especially as washing facilities might be limited for the next four weeks. With her heart-shaped face and even features, she guessed she would pass for pretty, but since Richard, she hadn't felt it. She deleted the photo and put her phone back in her pocket. She wondered what had happened to her lift.

Dr Brading had told her he would be passing through on his way up from London. If the coach had been on time, she would have had an hour to look round the museum before he was due to pick her up, but because it was late, she had thought she'd better stay put. It was now nearly half past three. She sighed. If she had known he was going to be late too, she could still have visited the museum as planned. She knew it housed an exceptional collection of pottery from the first century AD and wanted to get a heads-up on the type of material she might find on the site.

She had been really excited to be accepted on the dig Dr Brading was running. He was going to excavate what might be a Roman farm in the heart of the Iceni kingdom. He thought it may have been occupied around the time that the queen Boudicca led her revolt against Roman rule. If the dates were right, it would mean that at least one family in East Anglia had adopted all the trappings of a Roman life style really soon after the Roman invasion. This was unusual, but not unique in Britain as a whole, she reminded herself remembering the lectures she had attended about Fishbourne Roman palace just outside Chichester. What was surprising was the possibility of finding it was happening in a place where native opposition to the invasion was strongest. That was a real anomaly. She supposed that was the reason why Dr Brading, had managed to get a grant to cover the cost of the excavation. There was also a lot of interest at the moment in the way indigenous people were assimilated into the Roman Empire in the current global political context, so his pitch was spot on.

Gerry had found the Boudiccan revolt the most interesting part of her archaeological degree course at Bristol and loved the actual activity of digging, but she was also hoping that the practical experience could get her a job. The last two years had been a disaster – intellectually and personally. She shook herself mentally. That was all over. This was a new beginning, or would be if she could get started!

Where on earth was he? It had been his idea for her to take the coach instead of driving. He had emailed that the field where they were digging was in the middle of the countryside, so it was impossible to find, even by sat nav, and anyway pretty muddy so he had said there was no point in bringing a car. Apparently, there was a four-by-four for general use. That was going to be a bit of a challenge in itself. She'd never driven off road. Still, it was nice to know that he was the kind of bloke who had no equality issues and assumed capability rather than incompetence in women.

A beep from her coat pocket told her she had a message. She took out her smartphone again.

'A11 murder c u 5 museum entr'

Brilliant! That gave her time to look round the museum after all. She hoisted her rucksack over her shoulder, picked up her tent and headed for the city centre.

***

The pottery in the museum was amazing. Gerry had never seen such a variety. She loved the little barrel-shaped beakers. They were really cute and even had raised bands that she re-alised were meant to imitate the metal hoops that held the staves in place on beer barrels she had seen being loaded into pub cellars. She wondered if they were used to hold beer back in the Iron Age.

She was able to move freely around the exhibits, unen-cumbered by her luggage. Luckily, the staff on reception hadn't been too stuffy about leaving it at the desk – you never knew these days. She had visited Mont Saint-Michel in the spring when interrailing round Brittany, and they had closed the locker room due to heightened security. She had been forced to carry her tent and rucksack all the way across the bridge and up the steep cobbled approach, jostled by hordes of tourists, only to be refused entrance into the abbey.

She paused by one of the museum cases. Two gorgeous red goblets had caught her eye. The glossy surface made her think of Samian, the fine red tableware which was found a lot on Roman sites. She peered at the handwritten label on the shelf beside them. They were not Samian, she read, but Arretine ware from the middle of the first century AD, so earlier and much rarer. She admired the cherry colour of the goblets and the frieze of moulded figures that decorated the sides. It was a shame the label only gave the date but not who the figures were. She guessed the frieze told the story of one of the ancient myths. The label helpfully said that they had been found in the fort of Durobrivae. She remembered that was one of the earliest Roman forts in East Anglia. Maybe they had been bought into the country by a soldier in the Roman army, she thought, although, it would be a bit of a risk bringing such fragile pots in your luggage when you were coming all the way from Rome. She wondered what the journey would have been like for them. How long would it take? The last bit was obviously by sea but what about crossing France and Italy? They never told you this sort thing at uni – just about the pots and the coins and the remains of buildings. She wanted to know about the people that used the pots, spent the coins and lived in the buildings.

She heard a clock chiming outside and looked at her watch. Time to go. On the way out, she passed a diorama. Wax models were arranged in the middle of a room, part of a rectangular wooden hut with a thatched roof cut away so you could see inside. An artificial fire glowed on a central hearth and a man with matted grey hair and an unkempt beard was crouched next to it. He was dressed in a dirty white robe. Beside him was an open leather bag with a strange collection of metal implements spilling out onto the beaten earth floor. A very old man lay on a heap of furs on the bed in the corner next to the wattle and daub wall. Beside him sat a woman on a three-legged stool. Her face was arresting: hooded blue eyes, arched nose, thin lips, hollow cheeks and jutting chin that gave the impression of a bird of prey – a hawk, perhaps. Her red hair, streaked with white, was braided in two long plaits that hung down to her waist.

'Death bed of Prasutagus' read the sign in front of the scene.

Gerry smiled to herself. Of course, the woman was Boudicca, queen of the Iceni – the red hair and the hawk-like face were straight out of Tacitus – but what an unusual way to portray her. Most reconstructions showed her in a chariot leading the charge against the Romans. Only an incredibly perceptive and well-informed artist or his commissioner would choose to portray the moment at the beginning of the chain of events which set the rebellion in motion. She would have to find out more about this exhibit. She would ask Dr Brading who had been responsible for it.

Chapter 2

You could see the temple of the god-emperor Claudius every-
where you went in the town, a constant reminder of the con-
quest.

Tacitus Annals 14.31.12

Gwenneth's heartbeat slowed to a steady thud as the laughter
grew faint. She pressed her hands against the rough mud that
covered the walls, to steady herself. The shop doorway cast
deep shadows that had hidden her from the party of drunkards
roaming the streets of the Colonia. Not soldiers – they at least
were disciplined – but her own tribesmen, she had noted, and
her nose wrinkled in disgust. She wondered if Corin had
ended up the same way – drunk, dispossessed and wasting his
life. She had made enquiries everywhere but no one she spoke
to had any news of her brother.

She was beginning to regret agreeing to come on this
quest. Camulodunum was not the town she had imagined.
When she was a little girl, one of her favourite stories had
been about the emperor Claudius who had ridden through the
gates here on an elephant. The thought of seeing the place for
herself had been almost as exciting as the desire to find Corin,
but here she was at last, and it was turning out to be a disappointment.

She looked up across the roofs of the ramshackle wooden
huts that had sprung up to house the traders who had flocked
to the town in the wake of the Emperor's triumphal entry fif-
teen years ago. She could see the slender marble columns of
the Claudian Temple glistening in the moonlight. It had been
built to commemorate the Emperor's deification after his
death, and no expense had been spared. The marble had been

imported from Paros and carved by the finest Greek craftsmen. The statue of the god-emperor was solid gold. Only coin could buy such skills and materials, and Rome's newest province had only dogs, skins, wheat and wool to trade. Coin did not exist until the money lenders arrived.

Her father, Tinavu, had at first, like many others of his tribe, welcomed the alliance with Rome but the cost had proved high. Tinavu had been forced to go to the money lenders in order to fulfil the civic duties of Roman citizenship. Extortionate rates of interest meant he lost everything he owned and he was compelled to work in the new tile factory, a slave in all but name. The backbreaking work, poor conditions and meagre food left him weak and unable to withstand the sickness that raged through the living quarters.

Wet wool stroked her cheeks as she drew the hood of her cloak back from her face. The smell transported her back to one of the last times she had seen her father. He had just come home from a hunting trip, and she could picture him standing by the hearth, the raindrops beading his ruddy curls glowing like amber in the firelight. He was shaking his head like a dog and a spray of water sparkled like a rainbow as it caught and held in the smoke. He had bent down to scoop her up from her refuge behind her mother's skirts and swung her up in his strong arms high into the darkness below the thatch. Then he had clasped her to his chest and the rough fibres of his wet clothes had scratched the tender skin of her face. She was then only about four years old but remembered as if it were yesterday – the sharp fear followed by the sense of security conjured up by the musty odour of wet wool. How she missed him.

Gwenneth thought back to the day she arrived at Boudicca's palace with her mother, Gundred, and brother, Corin, after her father's death. The Iceni queen had been terrifying to a girl who up to then had known only laughter, kindness and love. Boudicca expected absolute obedience from every member of her household and Prasutagus had long ago given up any attempt to rule his tempestuous wife. At first, the bereaved family was so stricken with grief that they didn't care how their life was ordered, but as time went on, the continuous interference wore even Gundred down. It was not long before Gwenneth and her brother were orphans.

Corin couldn't bear it. As soon as he was old enough, he left to seek his fortune elsewhere. Boudicca had been furious. She had borne only girls and had looked upon Corin as the heir to the Iceni kingdom. From time to time, news of his whereabouts had reached them. Latest reports were that he was here in Camulodunum, and Gwenneth had been sent to fetch him home as Prasutagus was approaching death.

Gwenneth was startled from her reverie by the ringing of hobnail boots on the cobbles. Soldiers were coming. She was not afraid of them, but they would want to know what she was doing out here alone, and she had no answers she wanted to give. It was time to move on. She stepped out into the street.

A movement from an upstairs window in the inn opposite caught her eye. A young man was looking down at her. She could tell by his cropped hair and clean-shaven olive complexion, he was Roman. She drew her hood back over her face to hide herself from his gaze as much as to protect herself from the soft rain, which hung like a fine mist in the evening air. She turned to look down the street. On the hill to the south above the town, she saw smoke rising. If he was still the brother she remembered, that would be where she would find Corin. He would be living amongst her own people, not frequenting the taverns in the Roman part of the settlement. She hurried away.

***

Marcus turned away from the window as the slight figure rounded the corner and disappeared from sight. He wondered what a young native girl was doing here all alone. This part of town was fairly lawless since most of the troops had marched away with the Governor trying to quell the rebellion in the west. He had not been able to see her clearly through the rain, but her hair was a glorious colour and the confident way she moved suggested she was beautiful. She reminded him of his sister back in Rome. Little Pompeia was the same age, he guessed, but since she had put up her hair and donned the full-length tunic, she was forbidden to leave the villa without the escort of a family slave – and Rome was a good deal safer than this hellhole!

He glanced across at his companion. The older man was stretched out on the couch. The remains of their meal had not yet been removed from the table, but Quintus was idly tossing a pair of bone dice amongst the debris in some complicated game of his own devising.

Marcus studied his friend. The seamed brown face testified to many campaigns under the burning African sun. His thick black hair was starting to grey at the temples. It struck Marcus for the first time that Quintus was old. He wondered how the climate of this recently acquired Northern Province would affect them both and remembered, with a shudder, their hunting expedition into the eastern marshes the day before yesterday. Although it was early summer by the calendar, the icy wind had cut through his thick woollen cloak like a sword through yielding flesh and the mist had chilled him to the bone. Their hunt had not been successful, and they had dismissed the natives they had taken as their guides with only half the promised coin. The older one of the pair had shrugged philosophically. His younger companion had protested fiercely, but as Marcus didn't understand a word he was saying, he had not taken much notice. He didn't really care what the surly fellow thought of him. There was nothing much he could do after all. Time these natives knew what it was to be the conquered nation. This was The Roman Empire now.

Quintus looked up from his game. 'By all the gods, do you intend to pace the room all night?' He lifted the barrel-shaped beaker from the table. 'Come and sit down and try some of this beer.'

The younger man's face relaxed into a grin. 'No, thanks. I don't know how you can drink that filthy stuff. It's like everything else in this place – cloudy and cold and leaves a nasty taste in the mouth.'

He crossed over to a side table where a flagon of watered wine had been set and picked up one of the pair of glossy red goblets beside it. He traced the raised pattern of graceful floral scrolls and moulded figures appreciatively with his fingers.

'Only you, Quintus, would take the trouble to bring such fine Arretine ware as part of your luggage.' He threw himself down on the other couch. His finely marked eyebrows had drawn again into a frown. 'What in Hades are we doing here in such an uncivilised place?'

'I thought you were looking forward to this posting,' said Quintus mildly.

'That's because I thought we would see some action.'

'What makes you think we won't?'

'The fighting is over by all accounts apart from the odd skirmish in Siluria. Even the northern frontier is stable and from what I've seen so far, the natives seem pretty keen to ape the Roman way of doing things. You've only got to look at the temple here. It's really something.'

'Don't be fooled by appearances,' said Quintus. 'It's barely a generation since we took this province into the empire. Many of the natives who welcomed us then have been ruined paying for that temple you admire. Siluria is not the only region with malcontents. Tomorrow, it could be the Trinovantes – or even the Iceni – in rebellion, despite the treaties we have in place. We're sitting on a volcano here. My guess is it's only a matter of time before the whole place erupts.'

'So, you think we will see some action!' said Marcus sitting up.

Quintus couldn't help but smile, 'I'm sure you'll see more action than you could dream of, soon enough'

***

The clouds had parted to reveal the golden disc of the moon low on the horizon. In front of her, Gwenneth could see the entrance to the village of her tribe. She crossed the wooden bridge over the deep ditch and stood in front of the stout gates that barred the only gap in the high earth banks encircling the settlement. They were shut fast. She was reluctant to call out to ask for entry. She didn't want to shout out her business to a stranger. Disappointed, she started to turn away to spend the night in the shelter of one of the animal pens she had seen on her approach. A dog barked, and she heard the creak of the hinge as the gate was slowly opened. She turned back again and saw a weather-beaten face framed with thick gold braids. A pair of bright blue eyes studied her carefully. The stranger began to smile.

'Gundred?'

'Not Gundred, but her daughter, Gwenneth.'

'Little Gwenneth?' The stranger gripped her in a bear hug and almost swung her off her feet.

'It is me, Eisu. Your father's friend Eisu.'

In her mind's eye, a much younger face was superimposed on the face looking at Gwenneth and the two images merged. She smiled too then and was rewarded with another hug that drove the breath from her body. He let her go suddenly and grabbed her arm.

'Quickly! Come inside. It is dangerous here in the open.'

He drew here through the gate and into a nearby hut. The only light came from a fire blazing on the central hearth. Four great tree trunks supported the roof. Hurdles of wattle strung between these and the mud-coated outside walls broke up the interior space into four large bays, three of which were screened off from the central living area with lengths of woven cloth in rich earth colours of ochre, red and green. Above the hearth hung an iron cauldron suspended from a bronze tripod. Beside it sat a woman preparing wool for weaving. She was bent over her task, teasing out the coarse strands with a bone comb but looked up as Gwenneth and Eisu came through the leather drapes that sealed the entrance.

Gwenneth suppressed the cry that rose involuntarily to her lips as she moved forward into the circle of firelight and saw the woman clearly. She hardly recognised the young wife she remembered. A livid scar crossed the once-beautiful face from cheek to chin. The woman got up and filled a bowl with savoury stew from the cauldron. She handed it to Gwenneth with a crooked smile then went back to her task with her head bent forward so her black hair hung like a curtain to hide her disfigurement.

'Lolinda will bear that scar to her death,' said Eisu, noticing Gwenneth's shocked expression. 'It was the outcome of an afternoon's sport for a young officer. She got in the way of his target practice. His aim was not good and he caught her cheek instead of the sapling he was aiming for. He left her for dead. When I found her, she had lost a lot of blood and for weeks, her life hung in the balance. I went to the fort to ask for blood money but was turned away empty-handed. I suspect the young man was sent home to Rome and we will never be avenged.'

Gwenneth was confused. She had thought the Romans were well disciplined and not a personal threat to her people as individuals. The special relationship that her uncle Prasutagus had with the empire had led her to believe the Roman conquest had brought many advantages. Although her father had been ruined, it was the moneylenders he had blamed for his misfortune.

Eisu could see she was finding his story hard to take in. 'But these are old troubles. You will tell me in the morning why you have come so far, and why you have come alone. Now you can eat and rest.'

***

It was after midnight when Marcus left the inn. It was much later than he intended, but he had been reluctant to leave as it was the last night they would be together before Quintus went to join his legion. Marcus would be stuck here in Camulodunum on his own for a while. He had already discovered that there wasn't much for him to do whilst the governor, Paulinus, and most of the garrison were out on campaign.

He had been due to take up his appointment several months ago but bad weather had held him in Gaul whilst waiting for a passage across the sea to Britannia. In the harbour whilst making enquiries for the next ship, he had met Quintus who was also bound for the new province. The two men had immediately taken to each other despite the difference in their age and backgrounds. Quintus was on his second tour of duty in the north and had been sent to join the Ninth legion whereas Marcus was the son of a senator and had been sent by his father to join Paulinus as his assistant governor in preparation for a career in imperial administration.

Together, they had visited the seafront taverns, and Quintus had entertained his young companion with tales of his life on active duty in Africa. Quintus had found a captain willing to brave the spring storms and arranged a passage for both of them. He nursed his young friend through the violent sea-sickness that struck him as soon as they left port. When they finally reached Camulodunum, Marcus found that Paulinus had gone to deal with an insurrection in Siluria and left no instructions on what the young man should do in his absence. Quintus advised his new friend to stay put and offered to keep him company until his own orders came through. A very pleasant few days ensued as Marcus got to know the town and met some of the veterans who had retired there.

The moon had gone behind a cloud and it was pitch dark. Marcus did not notice the grey shadow that detached itself from the eaves as he set off down the street towards the barracks. The young Roman lurched from one side of the road to the other. He began to think the third flagon of wine had perhaps been a mistake. Then he became aware of the stealthy padding behind him. With a sudden burst of clarity, he realised there had been someone following him ever since he left the inn. He stopped and turned reaching for his sword then cursed as he realised that he was unarmed. He had slipped his belt off when they had settled down to some serious drinking. Quintus had already been asleep when he left or the older man would have reminded him that he needed to re-arm. A strong hand gripped him by the throat and thumbs pressed hard into his windpipe. A foul-tasting rag was thrust into his mouth. He began to choke on the fumes and his feet and hands went numb. Just before he lost consciousness he saw the glint of a knife blade.

Chapter 3

It is always raining or foggy in Britannia.
Tacitus, Agricola XII

Gerry came out of the door of the museum as the clock in the church across the park struck five. She looked around for Dr Brading, unsure how she would recognise him. He was coming from a meeting in London, so she was expecting him to wear a suit. She wondered where he would park as the archaeological collections were housed in the old castle and there only seemed to be pedestrian access through the grounds.

There was a dirty old Land Rover on the gravel in front of the entrance, and she could just make out the logo of the local archaeological unit through the mud on the side. Leaning against the driver's door was a man. Or rather, a bronzed god in cut-off shorts with bare legs and sandals (no socks, thank the lord, but cut-off shorts? On a man in his thirties?). His white shirt and rolled-up sleeves showed off a tan that rivalled the tans she had seen in Greece earlier in the summer. She felt distinctly overdressed in her jeans and jumper but was feeling the cold after weeks in the Mediterranean sun, although it was a lovely summer day. His dark hair was longer than most of his contemporaries but suited the whole hippie vibe and went well will the short beard – more 'today I haven't shaved look' than a beard. He was tall too – at least a head higher than Gerry, and she was on the tall side. He stood up away from the vehicle as she came closer and held out his hand.

'Gerry?' His voice was deep and he had a slight accent she couldn't place.

She held out her own hand and felt a slight jarring as he took it. Interesting, she thought. That hadn't happened for a while. His hand felt warm in hers.

'Yes, I'm Gerry Walker. I was expecting to meet Dr Brading.'

'The very same. Peter Brading, that is.'

Another small shock. She had been expecting someone older. This man was not much older than she was – and had got a doctorate, was senior lecturer at a first-class university and was running an excavation. It made her realise just how much time she had wasted.

'Dump your bag in the back and get in. We've got a couple of hours drive ahead of us. Have you had anything to eat?'

Gerry shook her head.

'Neither have I. We can stop at a diner on the way. The site is still under construction so to speak, so we won't have cooking facilities until tomorrow when the volunteers arrive and we start the rota off. The other staff may have already left for a meal in the village by the time we get back.'

Gerry felt a frisson of excitement at being described as "staff". She didn't really deserve it. She was really a volunteer, but because she had some experience, she had been taken on without having to pay the hundreds of pounds that was usually required. It had been amazing luck to get a place on a dig she didn't have to pay for considering how long it had been since she was last involved in archaeology.

They drove down the path to the main road. The pungent smell of mown grass rose from the manicured lawn as the land rover clipped the edges.

'Sorry about the wait. I had to collect the Land Rover from the depot and bring some finds up to the museum. Gave me a chance to change too. I couldn't wait to get out of the suit and get into my digging clothes. I hope you've got some old clothes with you too. It can get a bit muddy if it rains and dusty if the hot weather keeps up.'

Well, that explained the shorts and the Land Rover, thought Gerry. She had been wondering why anyone would drive such an unsuitable vehicle in such unsuitable clothes all the way from London. If he was making a delivery, it also explained why he had been able to drive right up to the entrance.

'No problem,' she replied. 'It was a great opportunity to see the types of pottery we would be finding over the next few weeks. I was also struck by the diorama at the entrance. Usually, you see Boudicca portrayed in the act of rebelling against Rome but most people don't know why. The Iceni were quite content to run a client kingdom, but it all went horribly wrong when her husband Prasutagus died, didn't it?'

'That's right. He didn't have a son so he had made Nero heir along with his two daughters. I think that set the fuse that channelled all the discontent you wrote about in your dissertation.'

Gerry felt a glow of pride. So, he had read her dissertation then. 'Who was responsible for the idea behind the diorama?'

'That would be me.' he said with a grin. 'I think we ought to treat our museum visitors with more respect and give them something to think about rather than dishing out the same old stories. Luckily, I am good friends with the curator, who is really receptive to innovation. We also have an ex-employee from Madame Tussauds who has retired to one of the outlying villages and is a keen member of the trust that runs the museum. By the way, did you get a chance to see the remains of the Claudian temple underneath the castle?'

'No, there wasn't really time.'

'That's a shame. Building it had a big impact on the native Brits. The cost was phenomenal, and it bankrupted the native chiefs – that and the establishment of the Colonia. The street we're driving over now was the main street of the veteran settlement. You can see the site of the original native settlement if you look behind as we drive up the hill. We're beginning to understand much more now about how these things contributed to the Boudiccan rebellion.'

'I know, I examined the evidence for my undergraduate dissertation,' said Gerry, wondering if he had read it, after all.

'Sorry,' he said with a laugh, 'I know you put all that in your dissertation, but I've gone into lecturing mode. I get so used to talking to students, both at my own university and the Americans who volunteer with me, who know nothing of the background.'

Gerry felt her cheeks grow hot. Why did she feel so antagonistic towards him? He was really nice and not a bit stuffy. She had got a bit sensitive to the possibility of mansplaining because of Richard. How had she put up with her old boyfriend for nearly two years, god knows. She changed the subject.

'Tell me more about the site and why we're digging there.'

***

The rain had been falling in a steady drizzle for several hours. Gwenneth was soaked through by the time she stopped at midday to rest her pony. A large oak tree on the side of the drove way provided shelter of a sort. She fished in her leather saddlebag for one of the bars of dried meat and fruit Eisu had packed to sustain her on the journey.

She would have preferred to return as she had come – by sea – but after much discussion they had decided it would be too risky. A young woman enquiring for a boat to Caistor was bound to attract attention. Eisu had lent her his favourite mare and enough food to last the three days it would take to get back home. She planned to break her journey overnight with some kinsmen who farmed a small holding just to the north of the new Roman fort at Durobrivae.

As she ate, Gwenneth thought about the previous day she had spent with Eisu. He had told her that nothing had been heard of Corin for many years and confirmed that her quest was hopeless. She had not been as disappointed as she thought. Whilst she loved her brother dearly, she could not see him in the role of client king. He was too headstrong. Eisu had suggested there was an alternative. There was a great deal of unrest amongst the local tribes, and he thought the young warriors would be willing to support Boudicca if there was a call to arms. The Elders still counselled caution but like dry tinder, only a small spark was needed to set the world alight. If Boudicca wanted to keep the Iceni free, she would not be short of allies.

Gwenneth was not sure about this alternative. From her experience, she felt that an unbridled Boudicca would be worse than the rule of Rome but she kept this thought to herself. Eisu had not been brought up in the royal household and wouldn't understand how she could possibly support the foreign invaders, as he saw them, against her own kin. Still, the information she had would placate her aunt and might make her homecoming a little less unpleasant. She hoped Prasutagus had rallied in her absence. If he had not, at least she'd had three days before she had to face the consequences.

The rain had stopped and the sun had come out by the time Gwenneth was ready to set off again. She was preparing to mount when she heard a strangled cry. It sounded like an animal in pain. She tied her horse back to the tree and went to investigate. A tangle of branches lay across the top of the ditch that ran parallel to the road. As she looked down through the leaves, she heard the sound again. This time, she recognised it as human. She struggled to clear the branches away. Beneath, lay a man. Not just a man, but a Roman. His cropped hair, olive skin and stubble were enough to identify him without the leather sandals and short tunic that revealed lean, muscled legs. Not only was he a Roman but he was the young Roman she had seen looking at her at the window back in Camulodunum. She wondered what could have happened in the intervening two days that had resulted in him being here and wounded pretty badly. The tunic under the red woollen cloak, once white, was stained rusty brown and she saw two deep puncture marks at his throat from which blood was still oozing. A horrible suspicion drew her gaze to his left hand. Her suspicion was confirmed. His middle finger had been sawn off. The bile rose in her throat. So, this was the way Boudicca had chosen to restore her husband to health. She turned away to retch. When she turned back, she found his eyes were open.

Marcus struggled to focus on the face swimming above him. He blinked, and the edges of the vision sharpened. He saw a tumble of tawny curls framing a perfect oval face, eyes the colour of sunlight dancing on a woodland pool, dark feathered brows meeting in concern over a delicate nose. Her mouth was wide and full and the colour of watered wine. She was lovely and strangely familiar.

He tried to sit up and found his head hurt like blazes. His hand ached strangely. He looked down and saw why and passed out. He came around again to the sensation of water dripping down his nose. He was propped against the side of the ditch, and the girl was wiping his forehead with a damp rag. His injured hand was bound with strips of cloth torn from his tunic.

'Can you move?' she asked.

He pushed against the side of the ditch and struggled to his feet. After several exhausting minutes, he managed to get a hold on a root and scrambled up onto the bank. He lay spread-eagled, breathing heavily.

'Try to get to your back against the tree,' she said.

Obediently, half crawling and half pulling against her warm body, he managed to sit. He was shivering. She held a bottle to his lips. The taste was sweet, almost sickly, and so unfamiliar, his first instinct was to spit it out, but he swallowed instead and felt the heat of the alcohol soothing his sore throat.

'Mead,' she said.

He recognized the word. It was the native name for fermented honey. Then realised that she had spoken to him before in Latin. He was trying to figure this out when two things happened at once. He remembered where he had seen her before and he remembered what had happened after he left the inn. He tried to get up. She put out a restraining hand.

'I must go now,' she said. 'I see there is smoke rising just over the hill. There must be a farm. I will leave word you are here and someone will come and pick you up and take you back to Camulodunum. You can keep the mead.'

'Don't leave me.'

'I must.' She had already mounted.

'At least, tell me your name.'

29

'Gwenneth,' she called back to him as she galloped away.

He slumped back clutching the bottle. She had recognised him too. Otherwise, how would she know he came from Camulodunum. He would find her again. He just knew it.

***

Several hours later, Gwenneth slowed her horse to a walk. She had called in at the farm as she had promised and persuaded the owner to get the young Roman back to the town in the interest of them all. If he went missing for too long, there would be reprisals and if he was returned, there might be a reward. Feeling she had done all she dared, she had ridden for miles alternating between a canter and trot to cover as much distance as possible before the Colonia was put on alert. It was obvious who was behind the attack to anyone familiar with druidic ritual – and there was bound to be someone with that knowledge in the pay of the Romans. Blood and flesh of a living man were needed to make a potion for someone gravely ill. For the magic to work, the victim had to die after the potion had been given to bar the path to the spirit world against the man they sought to cure. She had interfered in the rite and would be in serious trouble if she was discovered. She had been foolish to tell him her name.

At the farm, she had been more circumspect and had given a false name and pretended to be a camp follower. Nor had she mentioned the nature of his injuries – his hand was bound, after all.

She had felt strangely attracted to him and thought he might have felt the same. When she had glimpsed him two nights ago, she had thought him handsome despite – or perhaps even because of – his short hair and lack of beard. Even in the state he was today, the attraction remained – strengthened by the task of caring for him.

She shook her head to clear away the silly fantasy. He was a Roman and she was a Trinovante on her father's side and Iceni on her mother's, niece to the great queen Boudicca. There was no future for her in the world of a Roman soldier.

Still, it was unlikely they would meet a third time. She spurred her horse and trotted on through the afternoon, relishing the warmth of the sun and enjoying the unaccustomed freedom of riding alone.

The shadows were lengthening when she reached the road into Durobrivae. Circumventing the fort, she rode on towards the farm where she would stay that night. It was well hidden but Eisu's directions were excellent. The farmer, Bodwyn, and his family were glad to welcome a friend of their kinsman, and they spent a pleasant evening in storytelling and song. When she retired to one of the curtained alcoves, Gwenneth had almost forgotten her earlier fears and fell into a deep and dreamless sleep.

**

Marcus was not so lucky. His sleep was haunted by strange figures dressed in white robes drenched in blood. At least, though, he was in his own bed when he awoke the next morning, not dead in a ditch. The girl had been true to her word, and he guessed only an hour or two had passed before two taciturn young men had arrived in a wagon but it was nearing nightfall when they finally reached the barracks. He had been surprised to find how far away he was from Camulodunum. His attacker must have been pretty determined he wouldn't be easily found. He thanked all the gods that the girl had come along. There wouldn't normally be many travellers at this time of the year and no one would have thought of looking for him so many miles away from base. The road back to town had been little more than a rutted track. The wagon lurching from side to side coupled with the after effects of the drug made him feel sick. On his arrival, he had been seen by the army surgeon, who had shaken his head at the damaged hand. Tidying up the wound had been an ordeal. It was still possible that he could lose the rest of his fingers. He would have to wait a few weeks to find out. The neck wounds were fairly superficial but puzzling. None of the medical staff had seen anything like that or knew what weapon had been used.

It was a mercy it had been dry and cloudy for most of the time he had lain in the ditch and the branches that were meant to conceal his body had given him some protection from the rain that morning. If he had stayed there much longer, he would surely have died. Investigations were underway to discover who had attacked him and for what reason.

He wondered why the girl had been in such a rush to leave. What a beauty, though, with a wildness and vulnerability that had touched him in a way no woman had before. How tenderly she had wiped his forehead. He wondered who she was. She knew Latin, so was probably one of the chiefs' daughters. Well, whoever she was, he would find her again. He hoped she had not lied about her name.

Chapter 4

Buduica, was a Briton and more intelligent than most women.
Dio Cassius (Xiphilinus) 'Romaika' Epitome of Book LXII
Chapters 7–8

Throughout the night, Boudicca sat beside her husband and watched his chest rise and fall. The rhythm was uneven and slow. A rasp like the screech of a saw on wet wood punctuated each breath. She picked up the horn from the floor table and poured the dregs of the pungent liquid into his slack mouth but at that moment, he gasped for air. He gagged. She dropped the horn and raised his head as an oily stream of saliva dribbled through his matted beard. She removed her supporting arm and his head fell back on the heap of furs. She could see the whites of his eyes through his half-closed lids. The signs of approaching death were unmistakable. There was no longer any point in this vigil. She stood up and stretched out her arms to relieve the cramp in her shoulders. She felt the need to escape the confines of the sick room and strode through the hall and out the door.

The moon had lost its cloak of cloud and flooded the land with light. The royal palace stood on an artificial mound in the centre of the village. From this vantage point, Boudicca looked out over the open space of the mustering ground to the haphazard arrangement of huts that were the homes of her people. Some huts were too close together for a single pony to pass. Others stood alone, separated from their neighbours by large tracts of scrub, where the women went to dump the household rubbish. Dotted amongst the huts were animal pens.

In the distance rose the great defensive dykes, the massive earthworks that had, for generations, protected the settlement from attack by their enemies. Now, the enemy had changed. How could the dykes protect her people from the long-range missiles of the Roman army and the discipline of the legions? They could not, and if they were to survive, she must find some other way to deal with her former allies.

She turned her back on the village and mounted the two steps that led up to the great wooden door of the palace then paused on the threshold. The long hall was dimly lit by the red-gold embers that were all that remained of the fire in the hearth. In the shadows at the far end of the room, she could just make out the outline of an oak chair. It was there Prasutagus had sat to welcome the first embassy from Emperor Claudius thirteen years ago. Rome had needed help then to subdue the tribes to the north and west, and her husband had proved a good friend to the invaders. She remembered how the separate kingdoms had, one by one, been hammered into submission whilst the Iceni remained independent. Soon, even Siluria would be under Roman control. Imperial policy had changed with this success and autonomous rulers had no place now. The day would come when the Iceni too would be absorbed into the Roman Empire.

Her knees buckled and she reached out for the support of the tree trunk that held up the lintel. A splinter drove into her palm as the rough wood took the weight of her body. She winced and pulled herself back upright. She looked down at her hand. A bead of blood welled up, black against the whiteness of her skin in the moonlight. She raised up her hand to her mouth. The taste of metal felt good on her tongue. Her back straightened and her mind cleared. There was a way she could delay the inevitable for a while, perhaps even for her daughters' lifetime. She strode back to the room where her husband slept.

The sick man lay just as had left him, but instead of taking her place by his side, she paced about the bed. Every time he moved, she went to scan his face looking for a sign he was back with the living but his eyes remained closed. So, the hours passed until dawn when the druid returned.

'Where have you been?' she demanded.

He was startled to see the change in her. 'I thought we had agreed to begin the sacrifice.'

'Enough of that. We must rouse the King.'

'It will kill him.'

'He will die anyway. I need him awake, now.'

He knew that look and stopped trying to argue with her. 'At least, tell me why.'

'I want Prasutagus to change his will and make the emperor and my daughters the heirs.'

'Have you lost your mind?'

'It will flatter Nero and he is greedy. He knows we are wealthy and may leave us in peace.'

The druid shook his head. 'It is too risky. We should wait for the sacrifice to work. It will not be long now. The flesh and blood have been taken and will soon be prepared as the rite requires.'

'And if your magic fails?'

Two pairs of angry eyes locked in a battle of wills as the tall figures bent towards each other.

'Prasutagus will die,' said the druid and his gaze dropped to the ground.

Boudicca was triumphant. 'Then we will put it to the Elders,' she said, knowing he was losing his support as his powers failed and the old men would do as she commanded.

The druid made one last attempt to change her mind. 'If you convene the Council, it will warn the Romans.'

'It is too late for secrecy. Summon the Council.'

***

Boudicca sat in the great oak chair and looked around the circle of old men. The king's illness had been a closely guarded secret, and news of his approaching death had shocked them. There was silence for a few minutes. Then Anted got up to speak. He often put himself forward in situations where wiser men preferred to take their time before coming to a decision. His reputation for impulsiveness had lost him the status he felt he deserved even though he had achieved little in his life and was a poor speaker. He limped over to the hearth to take up the speaking rod.

'Why was this kept from us?' he shouted. 'We should have been told much earlier.'

'To ensure word did not come to the Romans before we had made plans for the future,' replied Boudicca.

'Do you accuse the Council of harbouring a spy?'

'You know as well as I do there are always those who will whisper secrets,' she said calmly. 'I did not even tell my daughters.'

The queen's air of command unnerved him and Anted returned the rod and scuttled back to his seat. He knew what she said was true.

No one else came forward to take up the rod. Boudicca gestured to the druid. He rose from his stool outside the circle and came over to stand in front of her on the other side of the hearth from the old men. His movements were hidden by the smoke as he drew a handful of dried leaves from the pouch at his waist and dropped them into the fire. It flared with a green light which rose from the hearth and flickered around him like an aura. A sweet odour spread through the air. The druid's shadow seemed to grow on the wall behind him. The Elders swayed to the rhythm as he began to chant.

'For thirteen years, we have been oppressed
Each year they take from us
The best cloth, the best corn from our harvest,
The best young men to fight for them,
The best young men to work for them
In salt mines, potteries and tile factories.
Our enemies grow rich as we grow poor.
The king will die.
The emperor will rule us.
We will be slaves.
It can be changed

We will make the sacrifice,
The living sacrifice.'

His audience was caught like a rabbit hypnotised by a snake, by the timbre of his voice and the intoxicating smoke and responded with a collective sigh. The druid continued:

The victim has been chosen.
He is young. He is strong. He is Roman.'
His listeners rewarded these words with a sharp intake of breath.
'Night falls, the moon is full, the star rises.'
The old men moaned in response.

'The searcher finds him and steals his senses.
The leeches bite and the blood runs free.'
They moaned again.
'The knife bites.
The cup is filled.
The meat is cooked.
The king drinks.'

'Yes,' they shout, 'yes', they shout again, and then a third time.
'The King lives!'
The chant ended with the druid's triumphant roar.
Boudicca remained still. The druid's body was blocking most of the vapour rising from the flames, and she knew the drug of old, so it had little effect on her.
'Enough!'
She rose from her chair on the dais and towered above them. Her voice had the effect of a bucket of water thrown on mating dogs. At her command, the fire was doused, more torches were lit and the leather flaps at the entrance were drawn back. A rush of cold air swept through the room and dissipated the lingering fumes, which had befuddled the old men. Instead of a powerful magician, they saw a dirty old man in a ragged cloak with greasy grey hair that straggled down to

his shoulders where it mingled with the matted strands of his beard.

In contrast, Boudicca was a warrior queen. She was taller than any of the men there. Her auburn hair, streaked with white, was held back from her face with a pair of intricately carved bone combs. A golden torc gleamed at her throat. Her strong features were cast into relief in the glow of the fire and her jutting nose and hooded lids gave her the look of a hunting hawk. Her eyes darted round the room and as her glance fell on each of the men, they felt their manhood shrivel. Once she was sure that she had their full attention, she sat down again to address them.

'Fools to think the might of Rome can be overcome by magic.' She looked down at the druid who was now squatting on the floor beside her. She looked up again. The old men shifted from one foot to another under her gaze, ashamed at the way they had been manipulated by a handful of leaves. Boudicca smiled to herself. It had been wise to let the druid speak first. Now that they had seen through his tricks and felt they had been taken in by magic, the old men would be easier to convince. She started with a deliberate attempt to shock them.

'Prasutagus must change his will. He must make the Emperor part heir and me the regent.'

This provoked an outcry, and Anted leaped up in protest. He was dragged back down by the men on either side and started muttering angrily to them and the others in the circle. Boudicca shouted across the noise. 'Silence!' Her voice echoed around the room. They stopped talking at once. Keeping her voice low and even to emphasise the logic of her plan, she carried on:

'Nero will be ruler in name only. He has problems all over the Empire that require his attention and will be glad to leave us in peace. We may even gain an advantage from the arrangement in reduced taxes. As the heir, he will be as interested as we are in keeping the kingdom prosperous. It will also play to his vanity, and he will be able to get political traction from using us as an example of how a nation is eager to voluntarily become part of the Roman empire because it brings such benefits.'

She looked around the circle of faces trying to gauge their reaction. Too much persuasion may lose the argument. She could see Anted was still hoping for an opportunity to challenge her again, but he was a fool and the others would not find his arguments persuasive. The older men would remember the effect of the revolt Prasutagus' cousin had had on their tribe twenty years before and would not want to repeat it. Satisfied that her will would prevail, she sat back and let the debate proceed.

One by one, the Elders came forward to take up the speaking stick. Caragon and Gorsa, as she had suspected, like Anted, supported the druid, but the rest were all with her. Once the debate was over and the decision was clear, she sent the druid to rouse the king.

***

Later that evening, a man was silhouetted by the setting sun as he limped across the scrub to a hut that stood on the western side of the village. At the threshold, he paused and looked behind to check that he had not been followed. He did not see the druid whose dark cloak blended with the shadows under the eaves. Anted pushed a small package beneath the skins that hung from the lintel to seal the doorway of the hut and limped back the way he had come.

The occupant of the hut picked up the package. He took two furs from the heap by the bed and wrapped one round his shoulders, securing it with a leather thong at the waist into which he tucked the package that had just been delivered. He threw the other over his arm. He drew the skins at the door back and slipped out into the night. He made his way to a wattle enclosure nearby, opened one of the panels and whistled softly. The sturdy shape of a pony loomed out of the darkness. The man took hold of the leather strap around its flanks and drew the pony outside the pen, closing the panel behind him. He flung the extra fur over the pony's back and leaped astride.

A few moments later, he was at the high gates that defended the gap in the dyke.

***

In the early hours of the next morning, a rider approached the entrance to the dyke at a gallop. He called out the password, and the huge gate swung open. He cantered through and up to the shrine behind the royal palace. The druid was outlined against the torchlight before the curtain swung back. The visitor handed the druid a metal flask and a leather bag. The druid turned away and held up the two objects in front of the three elders he had selected for their loyalty to him.

'Now the rite can proceed.'

'But the queen has forbidden it,' said Gorsa.

'No,' said the druid. 'She has made me rouse the king, and Prasutagus has changed his will, but she did not forbid me to carry out the rite. There is still a chance that my magic will save the kingdom from our enemies.'

The druid poured the contents of the flask into a barrel-shaped beaker. Then he opened the bag and extracted a bloody lump of flesh and splintered bone. He put it on the wooden table in front of him and took up a knife. The three elders watched him like frightened rabbits as he cut what had once been a human finger into tiny pieces and added them to the beaker. As he worked, he let out a strange high-pitched pulsing cry which turned into a rhythmic chant. The lamps flickered and dimmed and the druid seemed to grow in stature. The curtain that sealed the entrance to the shrine lifted and a cold wind blew through the room. A rusty red foam bubbled over the lip of the beaker. The chant became a prayer.

> '*Spirit of this flesh draw near.*
> *Bar the path.*
> *Bar the path*
> *To save our king.*
> *Camulos our god draw near.*
> *Drink this blood.*

40

Eat this flesh.
Bar the path.
Bar the path
To save our king.
Spirit of our king stay close.
The path is barred.
The path is barred.
The stranger dies
That the king might live.

As the druid finished, the lamps went out and the inside of the shrine glowed with a purple light. The druid picked up the beaker, ignoring the three old men who had fallen to their knees in front of him, their foreheads touching the mud floor, shaking with fear. He strode out of the shrine towards the palace.

Chapter 5

The Icenian king Prasutagus was famed for his wealth and longevity. In an attempt to keep his kingdom independent he made the emperor his heir along with his two daughters.
Tacitus Annals 31.1

Gerry woke early the next morning. She badly wanted a pee, but the sleeping bag was warm and it was a long way to the Portaloos. She reached for her mobile from the pocket in the tent wall by her head. 6 am. She didn't have to get up for ages. No message – no signal. They were well away from any masts. Strange to think she was in Norfolk, not far from the village where she was born.

That was an unexpected bonus. Her mother had always been pretty dismissive of the place, and Gerry had never thought to visit.

She had been surprised to find out where they were going. She hadn't really taken much notice of the actual location of the dig when Dr Brading – Peter, that is – had offered her a place. It had been set up by her old tutor at Bristol, John Goulding, who she had bumped into on her odyssey around the Greek islands. That meeting had been an amazing, and very lucky, coincidence. She and John had been the only two visitors to the Mycenaean palace on the island of Milos. They had shared a taxi back to the hotel in the port where they found they were both staying and later gone for a meal in one of the beachfront tavernas. It had made a nice change to have some-one to eat with, especially in Greece where the food is made for sharing. Over a litre of wine, she had confessed that she wanted to find a way back into research and study for a PhD.

He had agreed to help her but suggested she start by volunteering for an archaeological excavation so she could brush up on her digging skills. He remembered her dissertation had been on the Colonia at Camulodunum and had told her about the dig his colleague Peter Brading was planning for later that summer. John had explained he was now professor at the same university as Peter, so Peter had been prepared to take his word that she would be a worthwhile addition to his team. She had done a lot of digging in the past, so it wasn't exactly a lie.

However, the dig wasn't in Camulodunum in either the Colonia or the native settlement of the Trinovantian Tribe, as she and John had thought. It had taken two hours driving to get here, and she wondered why Peter had elected to pick her up from Colchester. She supposed it must have been so he could collect the Land Rover from the depot. She hadn't minded because it was interesting to see her home county. When she had told Peter that she had been born near where they were digging, he had joked about her red hair and Iceni ancestry. He had handed over the wheel for the last part of the journey so she could get used to the four-wheel drive. It was a bit old and clunky but fun to be up so high above the other vehicles.

Peter had explained the reason for the excavation when they had stopped to eat.

'We think we may have found a very early Romano–British farmstead,' he said, 'not far from what we are beginning to realise may have been the stronghold of the Icenians just before the rebellion.'

'Where was the stronghold?' she had asked.

'It's called Warham Camp,' he said. 'The location fits and the dates are right. What's intriguing though is the relationship of the farmstead to the fort.'

'I suppose you wouldn't expect there to be any Romanising influence in that area at that time.'

'Precisely,' he said as he sawed through what looked like a pretty tough steak.

Gerry had gone for the easier option of Chicken Caesar. She had declined his offer of wine and they were both drinking sodas but had accepted his offer to pay as funds were pretty tight right now.

'What evidence do you have for the date?' she had asked.

'There's been some pretty intensive field walking in the area and we have found some early military harness pieces. This type of evidence is unique for a domestic farmstead so far from the Colonia.'

Gerry went over the conversation again in her mind as she lay cocooned in her little tent. The campsite had been deserted that evening when they drew up at a row of caravans along the edge of a field. As Peter had predicted, everyone had gone off to the village for food, and he had disappeared into one of the caravans muttering he would see her in the morning, so she was left alone to sort herself out.

She had found a place to pitch her tent by the hedge on the opposite side of the field from the caravans where there were a few other small tents either side of a large marquee. She was glad her tent was so easy to put up as there was no one to help her. It just needed a twist and it unfolded all by itself. All she had to do was attach the guy ropes to the pegs and push them in. Luckily, the ground was soft enough as she hadn't thought to bring a hammer, and she didn't want to disturb Peter. There wasn't much to do, so she could see the attraction of going off site for the evening. She had felt self-conscious being outside on her own, especially as Peter would be able to see what she was up to from the safety of his caravan so she took refuge inside her tent and read until it was too dark to see.

It had been midnight when Gerry was woken by the other members of the team returning from the pub. She had checked her watch when she heard the giggling, which suggested at least some of the staff had been enjoying the local beer. After some whispering, they had all dispersed and Gerry had quickly gone back to sleep. Now it was morning and her first day of digging for two years. The need to pee was urgent. She pulled on her wellies and a jumper and crawled out into the cold.

* * *

Gwenneth left the farm the next morning when it was still dark. She wanted to get home before sunset. The first streaks of dawn had lightened the sky when she turned off the farm track to head east. She eased her pony from a fast trot to a walk and became lost in thought. She wondered how the young Roman was now. He attracted her in a way she couldn't understand. He was a stranger with olive skin, cropped hair and a shaven chin. Yet, somehow, he seemed more familiar to her than the boys of her people who she had seen grow into men with beards and long hair.

She remembered how his face had felt as she wiped the sweat away. The bristles had pricked her fingers and made them tingle. She had wanted to touch his lips and trace the shape of his mouth. It was the first time she had ever had such feelings. It had unsettled her and made her feel foolish.

How stupid she had been to tell him her name. It was because she somehow wanted him to find her again but that was impossible. What would be the point, anyway, she thought as she wiped away a tear and slumped in the saddle. Then she straightened up as a thought struck her. What if he should start asking questions about her? The druid might come to hear of it and work out that it was her who had interfered with his rite. She had put herself into real danger for the sake of an impulse. What a fool she was! Maybe the word was out already. She looked around the woods. Were those shadows moving in the trees just the effect of the morning sun or something more sinister? Her pony stopped, his ears twitching, and her heart started to race. He was as scared as she was. Could the spirits be abroad in daylight? Then she realised. He was afraid of her fear. She slipped down from the saddle, and he dropped his head and started to graze. She looped the reins loosely around his neck and stood a little apart until her legs stopped trem-

45

bling. When she mounted again her breathing was under control and the pony moved off at her command. She let her mind wander and found herself remembering every detail of her meeting with the young Roman: the shock of finding him; the surprise she had seen in his eyes when she spoke to him in Latin; his anger when she had left him by the side of the road; the way his body had felt against hers as she helped him struggle out of the ditch; the movement of his throat as he swallowed; the way his pupils dilated when he looked at her. Then this lovely image was replaced with one of gaping flesh and shattered bone where the knife had cut, and she felt sick. She rode on for many hours with her thoughts alternating between hope and despair. The late afternoon sun beat down on her back as she turned her horse east on the final stage of her journey and she was glad to reach the shelter of the forest as she drew near the edge of her aunt's kingdom.

***

Prasutagus was dead. Gwenneth could hear the women wailing as she approached the entrance in the great dyke. Her stomach tightened. The druid's magic had failed, and it was her fault. She prayed to Andraste to forgive her. Her fingers trembled as she dismounted and drew the hood of her cloak over her face. She left her pony tethered by the gate and continued on foot to the mustering ground.

The king's body lay on a wooden bier erected above a massive pyre. Around it, the women of the tribe were kneeling, tearing at their hair and beating their breasts. Gwenneth knelt on the edge of the circle in the shadows. She had no wish to face her aunt and her inevitable questioning or the druid until she had a chance to calm her nerves. She decided to stay with the mourners through the night.

Boudicca stood in front of the palace. She was stripped to the waist and her breasts and shoulders glowed blood-red in the setting sun. She watched in silence until the fiery disc had sunk below the horizon before she strode down to the pyre and seized a torch from the bronze tripod placed beside her husband. She held it high above her head then thrust into the centre of the wood beneath him. Wisps of smoke began to wreathe through the tangled mass of branches. Within minutes, the pyre was alight and leaping flames hid the body.

Boudicca re-fastened her tunic at the shoulders with crescents of solid gold and went back inside the palace. There, her daughters waited, recalled from their foster home to be told of their father's death. They were confused and frightened. Mardunad, the oldest, was just seventeen. Her sister Valda was two years younger. They had not really known their father as they had spent their childhood and adolescence away in the north. Their mother had told them her plans that morning, and they were terrified. Unlike her, they had no interest in politics or power and were timid and shy. They did not even look like her. They were short and dark like their father. Valda, although the younger of the two, had realised it was useless to complain, but Mardunad had wept until her mother lost patience and struck her viciously across the cheek. Boudicca then made them both stay inside, so they could not mourn their father properly.

By dawn, the flames had died and the pyre was a heap of ashes. The women had remained there all night. Boudicca brought the funerary urn out from the palace. It was a tall ovoid vessel with a flared rim and pedestal base. As she held it up, the dark burnished surfaces gleamed in the sunlight like polished silver. She stooped down and took up a handful of the ash and trickled it through her fingers into the jar which she then held up again.

'This urn holds the spirit of my husband, your king, Prasutagus. Through our feasting and ceremonies, we will give him passage to the spirits.'

The women dispersed to prepare the feast. Gwenneth was about to go with them when the queen caught sight of her. Her voice rang out in the still air. 'Come into the palace and choose a gift for the king.'

She turned and went through the door. Gwenneth followed slowly. She was exhausted from the long journey and all-night vigil, and afraid she might give herself away. Prasu-tagus had been no father to her, and she knew the queen had only used the gifting ceremony as an excuse to draw her inside. She wished she had stayed in Camulodunum. Eisu would have given her a home.

'Sit,' the queen commanded as she went to take her place on the carved oak chair. Gwenneth sat on the stool at her aunt's feet. Mardunad and Valda were already rummaging through the chests on either side of the hall looking for suitable items of gold and silver to bury with the king.

'So, you failed,' said the queen with a sneer. 'Maybe you can redeem yourself. Tell me, did you learn anything from your kinsmen in Camulodunum?'

Gwenneth, relieved to find she would not be punished, had no will to withhold the information Eisu had given her about the unrest amongst the Trinovante.

'So, the Trinovantes will be our allies,' said Boudicca when her niece had finished speaking. 'Perhaps, I should have let things be.'

Gwenneth felt the hairs on the back of her neck rise. So, her guess was right. Her aunt had initiated the rite of living sacrifice. That explained why she was not angry with Gwenneth for failing in her mission.

Boudicca got up and went to look at the shield Mardunad was holding up. It was made of leather, tanned dark brown, almost black and edged with silver. The central boss was made of gold decorated with sweeping curves and flourishes.

'Ah, this belonged to my grandfather. It is an excellent choice. Valda, find me a suitable sword.' She turned back to Gwenneth. 'Go now and prepare for the ceremony.'

Outside, the preparations for the feast that would take place after the burial were underway. Next to the remains of the pyre, the men had dug a pit. It had been filled with brush-wood, which had been set alight. By mid-afternoon, a layer of charcoal had formed. The women sat around the glowing embers gossiping whilst they ground grain. Four wild boars had been brought back by the hunting party and the skinned car-casses were roasting on spits over the pit.

By the evening, all was ready. Boudicca led a procession around the inside of the dyke carrying the urn containing the ashes. Her daughters walked behind her. Mardunad held the shield and Valda carried the sword. Behind came the druid carrying a cauldron, followed by the Elders, all bearing items of gold and silver they had chosen for their king. Next came the young men bared for battle and painted with woad, some with gifts of choice meat from the roasted boar. Behind were the women carrying bread and wine and cups and plates for Prasutagus to use in the spirit world. Gwenneth was amongst them carrying a pair of barrel-shaped beakers.

The procession completed a single circuit of the defences and reached the edge of a deep pit newly dug at the edge of the dyke. One of the warriors brought a pony wearing a richly decorated harness up to Boudicca. In one swift movement, she drew a knife from her belt and slit its throat. Blood drenched the front of her tunic, and the pony fell back into the pit. She replaced the knife and handed the urn to the young warrior. He put it between his teeth and climbed down a rope ladder at the side of the pit. The pony had fallen onto its side, and he carefully arranged its limbs with the urn by its head. Before climbing back up the ladder, he gave the pony a last pat on the flank – it had been his favourite mare.

It was then the turn of everyone in the procession to place their own gifts around the urn. Valda was first and sprang down into the pit with the sword, she had chosen, brandished in her right hand. She drove it into the ground next to the pony's muzzle and returned to her mother's side. Mardunad slung the shield across her shoulders and approached the edge of the pit. She started to climb down but had some difficulty negotiating the flimsy ladder and was red-faced and out of breath by the time she had laid her gift beside the sword and climbed back out.

After all the gifts had been placed, the younger men took turns to backfill the pit. When they had finished, the druid came to stand next to Boudicca and began to chant, calling on the spirits to welcome the king and accept the offerings they had made. His eerie cries made Gwenneth shiver. It did not do to linger too long between the dead and the living. She thought of the young Roman who should have taken the place of her uncle and shivered again. She wondered if he had survived the journey back to Camulodunum. He had lost a lot of blood and been out in the cold and rain for many hours. Then she remembered that the rite had failed. If Prasutagus was dead, the young Roman must be alive. Her breathing quickened. Maybe she would see him a third time if fate was kind.

Chapter 6

As long as nothing was done to injure their pride the people accepted both military rule and the burden of taxation imposed by our government.

Tacitus. Agricola XIII

Marcus relaxed against the side of the bath and let the warmth of the water loosen his stiff muscles.

His opponent had been experienced and cunning, and he had needed all this strength and skill to put up an acceptable show in the wrestling bout that morning. A delicious smell wafted through the bathhouse. Peering through the steam, he caught sight of the snack seller behind the colonnade carrying a tray piled high with spiced chicken legs. He was moving between the groups of old men seated on the wooden benches in the portico. The veterans liked to meet there to gossip and swap stories about their days in the army, and they would keep him in their midst for a while talking about their exploits, and he was content to wait for his lunch until the trader reached him. The rumble of their voices was quite soporific. He felt himself drifting into a pleasant daydream featuring the lovely native girl who had rescued him.

He was jarred back to the present by the ringing sound of hundreds of pairs of hobnail boots striking the cobbles in the outer courtyard. Marcus felt the tension rising in the room. Paulinus was away on campaign in Siluria and no troops were scheduled to arrive at the Colonia. What on earth was going on? Well, he would go and find out. He pulled himself up onto the tiles that surrounded the hot pool and strode off down the corridor taking a woollen robe from one of the slaves as he passed the changing area.

He found a messenger waiting for him back in his room. Orders had come for him to report immediately to the Procurator in the governor's office. He was surprised. The Procurator rarely travelled far from London. Something important must have happened to drag him this far north. Marcus chose a fine white linen tunic from the chest beside his bed and drew it over his head. It fell in soft folds to mid-thigh, revealing legs that were smooth and hairless from a daily scraping with olive oil and sand as part of his bathing routine. The neck and hem were bordered with purple – one of the privileges of belonging to the senatorial class. Around his slim hips, he fastened a leather belt with an ornate bronze buckle shaped like a horse's head, fumbling a little in his excitement. At last, he might have something to do in the governor's absence. He laced the thongs of his sandals, combed his dark hair, flung on a brightly coloured cloak and rushed out from his room to answer the Procurator's summons.

He found the Procurator, Catus Decianus, sitting at ease on a low couch, idly cleaning his nails with an ivory stick. Behind him stood two slaves. When Marcus appeared at the door, Catus waved languidly towards the table by the window.

'Fetch me a wine, dear boy…and I suppose you'd better bring one for yourself.'

Marcus was surprised to see two glossy red goblets that were almost the twins of those Quintus had brought with him from Italy, which they had drunk from in the inn. It gave him a comfortable feeling, and he felt more confident as he poured wine into one of the goblets and handed it to the Procurator. He filled the other one and sat down on the chair indicated.

'I hear you had a little accident,' said the Procurator.

Marcus instinctively covered his left hand with his right. The wound had healed but the missing finger had left a gaping hole.

'I was pronounced fit to return to duty yesterday.'

'Then I have a little job for you. I would do it myself, but I found the journey here somewhat fatiguing. I need someone to keep these slaves in order. They can be a little too enthusiastic in carrying out my orders.'

Marcus looked across at the two slaves. They were an unpleasant looking pair. The one on the left was a spindly fellow with an enormous pot belly. His head seemed too big for his body and the support of his scraggy neck. The other was very overweight. He had thick red lips, which he moistened from time to time with darting movements of his tongue. His eyes were almost hidden in rolls of fat. Marcus' evident disgust amused their master.

'Meet Epillicus and Lemnus, my faithful servants. Now, down to business. My spies tell me that Prasutagus is dying – well, he may be dead already – the news is a few weeks old. You know who Prasutagus is – or was?'

'Of course.' The young man bridled at the assumption he wasn't familiar with the names of the native rulers.

'What you won't know is that in a foolish move to prevent the kingdom losing its independence, the king on his deathbed made Nero his heir.'

'Why? How would that help? Surely, it would make it easier to take the kingdom back under our control?'

'Yes, I fear they have miscalculated,' said the Procurator draining his goblet. He gave it to Epillicus to refill. 'I should clarify. Nero was to be part heir with the two daughters and the wife as regent. I suppose Prasutagus thought the emperor would be too busy to trouble himself with a client kingdom so far from Rome and leave the wife – Boudicca – to carry on as ruler. But that wouldn't suit us at all. It would set a bad example to the other tribes. And we mustn't forget all the gold and silver which, as part heir, Nero is now entitled to. So much more valuable than the measly taxes we extract. So, now you have probably realised why I am here.'

Marcus looked back at the Procurator. His mind was racing but he kept his expression blank.

'You don't? I am surprised – a smart boy like you. We are going to take what is owed to Nero. My slaves will be responsible for seizing the appropriate value of goods. In case of resistance, I have brought troops with me. You will go with them to represent me and the governor.' His eyes rested on the purple borders on Marcus' tunic. 'The son of a senator is a fitting ambassador. Be ready to leave tomorrow at dawn.'

Marcus left with his head in a whirl. He was glad to have something to do but had doubts about the nature of the job. That poor queen, only just widowed and having all her wealth taken along with her independence. It seemed pretty unjust. There was nothing much he could do about the outcome, but maybe he could use his influence to make sure that Boudicca and her daughters were treated with kindness and respect.

***

When Gerry finally emerged from her tent on her first morning, she almost tripped over a tape stretched taut across the entrance. She recovered her balance and looked up to see a young man of around her age. His brown eyes were alighting with laughter.

'Loving the Bambi homage,' he said.

She had no idea what he was talking about at first then realised he meant her Disney pyjamas, which were revealed in all their childish glory between the top of her wellies and the bottom of her jumper. In her hurry to get out to the Portaloo – she really had left it too long – she hadn't thought to put on her jeans. She felt the blood heating her cheeks and mentally cursed her adolescent tendency to blush.

'No worries,' he said. 'My own taste is for Toy Story.'

She had laughed even though the joke was a feeble one.

'My name's Tom, by the way. I'm just measuring in the grid. If you go to the blue and white caravan when you have washed and dressed, my girlfriend Annie is making breakfast.'

Annie greeted Gerry with a smile. She cooked some fresh bacon for Gerry to make a butty with lashings of brown sauce.

'I'm managing the finds,' she said. 'We can have a chat later, but I need to get all the trestle tables set up and the trays unpacked. We probably won't find much today but I want to be ready just in case. Roman sites turn up so much material I'm likely to be run off my feet in a couple of days.'

She left Gerry to eat on her own and disappeared into the marquee.

Just as Gerry was finishing her second cup of black coffee, Tom came over to the caravan carrying a spade.

'Looks like you and me will be taking the turf off by ourselves until the volunteers turn up. Paula and Daniel, our geophysicists, will be putting up the shed and unpacking the tools they brought from the depot yesterday. Peter and Anthony – you'll meet Anthony later – are sorting out the paperwork in the office – that's the green and white caravan in the row. Have you done this before?'

'Yes,' she replied, 'but not for a long time. Do you mind if I do the cutting and scraping? I don't have the stomach muscles yet to cope with the shovelling and barrowing.'

'That make sense,' he replied. 'Let's get started.'

Half an hour later, the volunteers began to arrive, turning up in ones and twos. They were staying in a hostel in the village only a mile from the site but Gerry noticed they were all out of breath and pretty red in the face. It was hardly surprising, she thought, as most of them were on the large size and looked as if they weren't used to exercise. There were ten of them in total. All Americans who had only flown into London the day before, so not only overweight but jet lagged.

She supposed they were here to get credits for their university course. They gathered in front of the marquee to get their first briefing from Peter. Gerry used their arrival as an excuse to stop and to catch her breath, resting on the spade she had been using to cut through the roots whilst Tom pulled at the turf roll.

After the briefing, the volunteers were assigned to help remove the turf but none of them seemed to be able to use a spade, so in the end, Gerry and Tom worked down opposite ends of the trench doing the cutting while the volunteers took turns to pull the turves free and carry them to the far end of the field, where they made them into a wall which would eventually contain the spoil heap.

They stopped at midday for lunch. The volunteers had sandwiches provided by the hostel, but Annie made soup with bread and cheese for herself, Gerry and Tom. The three of them ate together in companionable silence. Paula and Daniel had gone off to the depot to get more equipment and Peter and Anthony remained closeted in the office.

They had another break in the afternoon. Annie made tea for everyone, which they drank by the mess caravan. It had been time to finish for the day before the last of the grass had been lifted in the roped off area. The volunteers trooped off back to the hostel. Gerry crawled on top of her sleeping bag and collapsed. She hadn't done any physical work for ages and de-turfing was a killer. The shadows lengthened.

'Dinner's ready,' called Annie.

Gerry didn't hear. She was fast asleep.

Chapter 7

It started when Boudicca his wife, was whipped and his daughters were raped.

Tacitus. Annals 31.4

Boudicca stood on the top of the dyke and watched the soldiers arrive. She did a swift calculation. The reports had been accurate. There must be around two hundred and fifty men, three centuries. Behind them trundled three wagons drawn by pairs of bullocks. This was not a friendly visit. The Romans must have been preparing in advance. It was only three days since she sent the message to Londinium. A traitor? She had suspected a certain member of the Council for a long time now. Well, he would be dealt with. Now, she had more urgent problems to address. It looked as if her plan had failed. If only they had more time. She did not have enough warriors to fight this army. She gave the order to open the gates and returned to the palace. For now, she would have to comply with whatever Rome wanted but later – well, they would see.

***

Marcus was tired and uncomfortable. The journey had taken longer than he thought. There were no good metalled roads in this part of the province and the wagons kept getting bogged down. Discipline had been a problem too. Decianus' men were either unused to active duty or had been side-lined because of their incompetence. As the leading wagon had turned into the track leading to Boudicca's stronghold, the driver had taken the corner too fast and it had ended up in the ditch. The other two had crashed into it and it had taken hours to disentangle the vehicles.

Marcus was worried about how it was all going to end. He had heard through the grapevine that Decianus had promised the soldiers a bonus to encourage them to march this far north. He was worried that this effectively gave them a licence to loot. He was thoroughly disillusioned by the whole expedition. He decided when the business with Boudicca was over, he would not return with Decianus' men but go in search of Quintus, who was stationed nearby. Anyway, they were here at last and thankfully, the gates stood open. Perhaps, the native queen would comply and all would be well.

***

Boudicca sat on the oak chair in front of the hearth. Mardunad and Valda sat on a sheepskin at her feet. The Elders stood in a circle behind. The druid sat at her side. Gwenneth leaned against the wall at the far end of the hall, outside the circle of light cast by the torches. Marcus was the first to enter. Gwenneth recognised him at once and moved further back into the shadows. The druid noticed her withdrawal. He looked closely at the young Roman. His eyes narrowed as he noted the missing finger on his left hand. So, his magic had not lost its potency. The girl had something to do with this. He would deal with her later.

Marcus had focused all his attention on the queen. Not a weeping widow but a formidable warrior. She sat upright with her head held high. Auburn braids shot with silver almost reached the floor. Her eyes were a piercing blue and cold as ice. She looked like a hawk with those eyes and beaked nose.

'State your business.'

Her voice was as deep as a man's. Marcus stumbled through the opening of the speech he had rehearsed. He was pushed aside.

'We have no time for this,' said Epillicus. His jowls quivered as he waddled up to the hearth. 'You know what we've come for, lady. Show us your treasure.'

58

Boudicca rose to her feet, shaking with anger. 'How dare you address me this way? I am a trusted ally, a loyal friend to Rome.'

Epillicus wasn't listening. He had seen the oak chests that lined the room. He beckoned to Lemnus, who was waiting by the door. The skinny slave hurried over, and one by one, they threw back the lids and began rummaging through the contents. Piles of gold and silver objects tumbled onto the floor. For a several minutes, everyone, including Boudicca, was stunned into inaction by the spectacle. Then, recovering from the shock, she strode over to the chests and started slamming down the lids. Epillicus was slow to move, and his hand was caught in the hinge. He screamed in pain.

'Seize her,' he shrieked. Two soldiers came running up and grabbed her by the arms, twisting them roughly behind her back.

'Tie her to that post.' He stripped off his girdle and flung it at the nearest soldier, indicating one of the four tree trunks holding up the roof.

Marcus felt helpless as the slave took command. Within a few moments, Boudicca had been tied to the post by the wrists with her arms high above her head, her face pressed against the rough bark and her tunic ripped from the pins that held it at the shoulders to expose the ivory skin of her back.

'Now, clear the room and ring the palace with the troops.' He pointed to Mardunad and Valda, who were cowering on the ground clasping each other tightly. 'You can leave the girls.'

The Elders were hustled out like frightened rabbits.

'Fetch a rope.'

Marcus was appalled. 'You can't do this,' he stuttered.

'I most certainly can,' said the slave. 'This is not the governor's business but the Procurator's. This woman assaulted me in carrying out the orders of my master. She must be punished. You can stay and watch or you can leave but don't try to stop me. The soldiers are under my command not yours.'

Marcus was forced to stand by helplessly as the horrible drama unfolded. A soldier returned with a rope and handed it to Epillicus. The slave tied a knot in the end. He stroked the knotted rope along the length of Boudicca's spine then raised his arm and struck. The tempo and frequency of blows increased until the creamy skin was broken and bleeding. He did not stop until the flesh looked like a lump of raw meat. Throughout, the queen made no sound, but by the end, her legs no longer supported her and her wrists took the whole weight of her body. Marcus kept his head lowered and his eyes closed but winced with every sickening thud.

Lemnus was too preoccupied with his search for treasure to take any notice of the flogging. He had been making his way steadily down the room, rifling through each of the chests in turn. A pile of choice pieces of the treasure was accumulating behind him: golden torcs, shields, swords, mirrors, brooches, even gold coin. Gwenneth trembled as she watched his approach. Her discovery was inevitable unless she could slip away into one of the curtained alcoves. When Lemnus seemed to be distracted by a particularly beautiful piece of metalwork, she moved cautiously out of the corner, bent over double to make herself less noticeable. But the slave was not absorbed as he seemed.

'Well, well, what have we here?'

Gwenneth screamed as she felt his bony finger grip her thigh. Marcus turned around in alarm. Even though the edge of the room was dark, he recognised the girl who was caught in the slave's arms. He rushed up to the struggling pair.

'Take your hands off her,' he shouted as he ran.

'So, you want to play now,' sneered Lemnus. He thrust the girl into the boy's path. Marcus stumbled, lost his balance and collided with Gwenneth. The force knocked her over and he fell on top of her. She tried to scream again, but the weight of his body had driven the breath from her lungs. She went limp. His arm tightened about her.

'Trust me,' he whispered.

Her heart was beating fast beneath his own. 'Please help me,' she whispered back.

He nodded and rolled them both into the curtained alcove she had been trying to reach. He felt the softness of the furs used for bedding against the back of his legs and piled them over the girl, who was now shivering uncontrollably beside him. He made as if to get up but she pulled him back.

'Don't leave me,' Her words were barely audible.

He lay down beside her again.

Lemnus walked back to join Epillicus who was splayed out in the oak chair, exhausted from the unaccustomed exercise and nursing his swollen hand.

'That boy's given me an idea. How about a bit of fun with the girls?'

He went over to Boudicca's daughters, who were clinging to each other in terror. Valda whimpered as he forced her head back by tugging at her braid. He ran his nails down her throat and through the opening at the neck of her tunic. He found her left breast and squeezed it hard.

'This one's too small for me.'

Epillicus looked up.

'I'll take her. I like a neat little handful.'

He got up from the chair and flopped down on the sheepskin on top of Valda. The breath was knocked out of her and she lay passively under the rolling mountain of fat. He tore at her tunic and pushed into her. He came with a high-pitched moan within seconds. He lay still for a few minutes then struggled to his feet. Blood stained the white wool beneath the girl.

'A virgin. That's a bonus,' he said with a satisfied grin. He waddled back to the oak chair.

Lemnus caught hold of Mardunad's foot as she tried to edge away. He thrust his hand up between her thighs. She bit him on the arm.

'Bitch!' He punched her savagely on the side of the head, knocking her out. He turned her onto her front and entered her from behind. He grunted as he thrust over and over again into her still body.

'I need more resistance,' he said at last.

'Try the other one,' then said Epillicus. 'Young Marcus should have finished with her by now.'

Marcus had been listening in disgust to the sounds coming from the other side of the alcove. His honour demanded he do something to help those poor girls, but he hadn't dared to leave Gwenneth unprotected. Now it seemed they would take her too. He thought quickly.

'We have to pretend I am raping you,' he whispered.

She looked up and nodded. He saw the fear in her eyes and gently touched her lips with his own. He meant only to reassure but sensation exploded in his mouth as their tongues met. Within moments, they were lost in the storm of passion that was unleashed as their bodies responded to each other. They didn't even hear Lemnus snort in derision when he looked into the alcove.

'That young man certainly has stamina,' he said when he returned to Epillicus. 'Looks like the skinny one will have to do.'

***

Gerry stood on top of the inner bank. Peter had brought the volunteers to Warham Camp on their day off to explain the context of the site they were digging and she had elected to come too. He was down with them in the centre of the hill fort that he was convinced had been Boudicca's stronghold. She had left when he started telling them about Boudicca's flogging and the rape of her daughters. It made her uneasy, and she didn't want to hear what he had to say about it. The horror, pain, shame – the way it must have affected the women – seemed to be unimportant to modern historians who seemed only interested in the events as a trigger for what came next. Tacitus, who was writing pretty well immediately afterwards in the scheme of things, had thought the event warranted only a couple of lines.

Gerry tried to put herself in the place of the queen before it all happened. Her husband had just died. Would she be grieving? Did she love him or was that an alien emotion in those ancient times? Would she have stood here too, up on the inner bank where Peter had said there was a timber walkway, looking out over the palisade fence beside the entrance, watching the Roman troops arrive. Would she have been

62

frightened or defiant? Would she have suspected such treachery? Would the rebellion still have taken place without that provocation? Sadly, these were not the questions archaeology could answer. How amazing it would be to go back in time and understand why. Contemporary accounts, like the Annals of Tacitus, were more likely to be propaganda than truth. Imagination was all you had.

She looked out over the valley. It would have been wooded then as far as the eye could see. Two thousand years ago, there would have been a track right up to the entrance just as there was now. Two hundred or more soldiers would have stood outside. Maybe there would have been wagons with provisions – it was a long march from London – and they would need wagons to carry back the treasure they were planning to loot. She was sure Boudicca would have stood there alone, leaving her daughters in the palace. What would that have been like?

She dragged her mind away from those long past events and turned to look at the inside of the hill fort. Peter had said that it had never been excavated. She knew that most Iron Age houses were round with conical thatched roofs and walls of wattle and daub and pictured them dotted around the space enclosed by the high banks. She remembered reading that high-status houses were rectangular and she imagined the one Boudicca lived in would have been somewhere in the centre. There might be cremation pits as well as houses. Perhaps even the one where Prasutagus was buried. She turned back to look out over the Norfolk countryside again.

'Great view, isn't it?'

Gerry swivelled round and smiled at Peter. He was standing a few feet away from her.

'I was just wondering how Boudicca would have felt as she watched the Roman soldiers arrive.' She could see he was about to start lecturing her about the events that followed and hastily changed the subject.

'Do you think Prasutagus could have been buried here in the fort?'

'Interesting question. There are a few areas of disturbed ground that could be cremation pits. I hope to come over here with Anthony next week. He wants to do some dowsing.'

'Dowsing? That sounds pretty unscientific. What can you find with dowsing on an archaeological site? I thought it was the hippy dippy way to find water.'

'Don't let Anthony hear you talking like that. He has a great record. Don't know how he does it, but he's as good with his rod sometimes as a geophysicist is with all his fancy equipment. Time to go now though. The volunteers have a meal booked in the hostel at 6 o'clock.'

They walked together to the end of the dyke where there were footholds in the inner bank next to one of the modern entrances. Peter went down first and reached out to help her at the bottom, where rainwater had collected making it slippery. Once again, Gerry felt a little shock as their hands met. She looked up, but he was watching the volunteers trailing off down the track back to the main road where the Land Rover was parked and seemed to have noticed nothing.

***

Gerry's heart was pounding. She thought the nightmares had stopped for good. They had happened so often at one time that she used to try and find a safe place before she let herself fall asleep. In her last waking moment, she would scan the bedroom planning how to get into the cupboard at the top of the wardrobe when the lion stalked through the door. It was usually a lion that she was running from. In a tent, there was nowhere to hide. But on the other hand, there was the comfort of people being around. She could hear a soft snore a few yards away. Maybe that was the source of the dream. A friend had told her that in dreams, everything was a part of you, so she had wondered what part of her she was trying to escape from.

As her heartbeat returned to normal, she ran through the events of the day trying to identify what had disturbed her.

The trip out to Warham Camp had been great. It was a beautiful day, and she had sat in the front seat of the Land Rover Peter was driving. It had been more fun talking to him this time. They had the shared experiences of the dig, so it was more like a conversation than the monologue she had been subjected to after he picked her up from the museum. The familiarity of daily living – eating outside the mess caravan every evening, passing on the way to the loo in the morning, chatting about this and that in the pub on the few occasions when he joined the rest of the team – had made them easy with each other and silences were no longer awkward. What was awkward was the sensitivity she had to any contact, even when he touched her in the most casual way. The question was – what was she going to do about it? If she slept with him, he might think it was because she wanted his help to get a job in the university. Worse, he might think she was fair game because of her ambitions? He seemed like a decent bloke but so had Richard. Then, what if things went wrong? She didn't think she could handle a casual affair and the pain of being dumped again. She wished she could be more relaxed about relationships, but her experience to date seemed to be hampering any hope of future happiness. Perhaps she was over-thinking this. Maybe she should just let events take their course. She snuggled back down in her sleeping bag and tried to relax, but it was nearly dawn before she finally fell asleep.

Chapter 8

The legion was routed by the Britons. Every one of the infan-
try was killed but Cerialis escaped with the cavalry and took
refuge in the fort.

Tacitus. Annals 32.13-14

Gwenneth carefully lifted the arm that lay across her breasts. Marcus stirred in his sleep. She held her breath and waited. He turned over and settled back into the furs. She crept out from the alcove. There was no sign of her aunt or her cousins or the slaves who had violated them. The druid was sat in the oak chair, waiting for her.

'I saw the way you looked at that young Roman,' he said. 'You know him. You have lain with him – willingly.'

Gwenneth was silent before his accusation. She was as in-nocent this morning as she was the night before but the es-sence of his words was true.

'I saw his hand,' the druid continued. 'You have been very foolish, foolish and guilty of killing the king. You should not have interfered. What happened here is your fault.'

His coldness was worse than his anger.

'I did not know, please forgive me.'

'You are lying. His wound was unmistakeable. You are twice traitor. Traitor to the spirits and traitor to your tribe.' He rose from the chair and took a glowing branch from the hearth. 'Now all our people will know what you have done.'

He swung at her head with the branch. It caught her on the temple. She ducked under his arm and ran for the door. The druid came after her screaming curses. She sped down the slope beside the mustering ground and into the gaps between the huts that lined the dyke, through the entrance and out onto the driveway. She dived off into the woods, twisting and turning through the trees until she was sure she had lost him. She collapsed on the ground sobbing for breath. The burn was agonising. It would leave a terrible scar. By that scar, everyone she knew, and strangers she had never met, would know that the druid had banished her for her treachery. There was nowhere she could go and no one who would shelter her.

**

Marcus dreamed that Gwenneth was trapped in a fire. He could smell burning flesh. Her screams tore at his heart but the heat of the flames drove him back every time he tried to reach her. He woke in a panic and reached out for her body. She was gone. He threw off the furs that were stifling him and struggled to his feet. He stumbled through the gloom of the empty hall into the daylight. There was no one about. The troops and the wagons with their loot had gone. He realised he had no idea where to find the girl. She could be in any one of the huts but he dared not go searching for her. Word would have spread about the outrages of the night before. Without military support, he was an open target.

He walked around the palace towards the dyke hugging the walls to avoid being seen and found his horse had been left behind, hobbled to prevent it straying. Grateful for this mercy, he quickly mounted and rode out through the open gate. For the first time in his life, he felt ashamed to be Roman. He started off on the road that led back to Camulodunum but turned back after a few minutes. He had no stomach to face his former comrades right now. Instead, he galloped off in the direction of Durobrivae. He needed the sanity of his friend Quintus.

**

The druid returned from his fruitless pursuit. He went behind the palace to the shrine. Inside, Boudicca lay face down on a raised platform. She raised her head as he entered.

'I heard screaming,' she whispered, unable to speak normally because it hurt too much to breathe. 'Are the soldiers raping more of our women?'

'The soldiers have gone,' he replied. 'They left at dawn. It was Gwenneth you heard.'

'Gwenneth? If the soldiers have gone what happened to make Gwenneth scream?'

'I branded her,' he replied drawing closer to look at her back. He had coated it with a thick paste to soothe the pain and heal the torn skin. He would need to apply more soon. He could tell by the way she was holding her breath that the numbing effect was wearing off. He went around the platform to check on his other patients. Mardunad and Valda were curled up in each other's arms sleeping deeply. He nodded to himself. The herbs in the potion he had brewed had a powerful narcotics effect and would soothe their minds and bodies.

'By whose authority?' Boudicca demanded.

He turned and looked at her dispassionately. At last, he had her in his power.

'I needed no authority but my own. Gwenneth had dared to interfere with my magic. Now I have branded her, and she is no longer one of our tribe or protected by our gods.'

Boudicca rested her head back on her arms. She was in no position to argue with him. She needed him to help her heal. Then they would see.

'Tell me what she has done to deserve this punishment.'

He told her.

***

'There was nothing you could do, my dear boy,' said Quintus when Marcus had finished talking. 'You mustn't blame yourself.'

They were dining together in the old soldier's room. Marcus had arrived at Durobrivae the previous day, white and shaken. Quintus had been shocked at the change in him. He had noticed the missing finger and it had puzzled him, but he decided to say nothing until his young friend broached the subject. That had not been until tonight. Marcus had spent the day out riding whilst Quintus was occupied with military matters. When they had met again that evening, his natural good spirits had been restored. After a light supper of bread, cheese and fruit, Quintus refilled their mugs. Marcus had got used to the native beer and had been surprised to find it was actually more refreshing than wine. The old soldier settled back amongst the cushions on his wooden couch and watched his young friend, who had got to his feet and was wandering around the room, picking up and examining the bits and pieces Quintus had acquired on the journey over to Britannia.

'I see you still have the Arretine goblets,' he said and returned to his place at the table. Handling the smooth tableware had reminded him of that night at the inn when he had first seen Gwenneth but also of his meeting with Decianus. At last, he felt ready to speak. While he told the story of the last few days, Quintus listened in silence, appalled by the way the affair had been handled. Catus Decianus had clearly used the boy to shield himself should there be any repercussions. It was highly likely the slaves had been given full licence to behave as they did – and the Procurator would have known of their proclivities. It was also entirely possible he had actually ordered the flogging. Marcus felt a great sense of relief now it was all out in the open.

'There is one thing that puzzles me,' said Quintus. 'What was behind the loss of your finger?' He thought for a moment. 'I once heard of a similar case of mutilation. I think it was in Gaul. The victim was found dead from loss of blood and exposure some days later.'

'I would have been dead too if it wasn't for the girl.'

'You said she was frightened when she rescued you.'

'Yes. I couldn't understand it. The attack had happened miles away and two nights before, so the attacker was long gone and she was perfectly safe. Yet, before she knew that, she wasn't too frightened to help me when for all she knew my attacker was still lurking where she found me.'

'Did you talk to her about it when you met again at Boudicca's palace?' He saw the look on his young friend's face. 'I know, I know, that was a stupid question. So, what will you do next?'

'About the girl? I don't know. I can't really go looking for her amongst the Iceni. They won't be very happy to see a Roman again for a very long time.'

'I meant about the atrocities. The governor should be told. Do you have any idea when he plans to come back east?'

'None at all. Maybe I should go and join him. I should be able to find someone back at Camulodunum who is willing to guide me. There are a lot of young Trinovantes hanging about there looking for work.'

'That might not be such a bad idea – going to see the governor, although, I think you should avoid taking on a native guide after the events you have described. You might be better off travelling alone. I can give you a map which shows the main roads through this province. Most of them have inns and staging posts where you can get a bed for the night and change your horse. You would need to keep your wits about you, though. You've been caught out once already and lucky to survive.' He noticed Marcus' quick glance down at his hand. He needed to take the young man's mind off the events of the past few days. 'Come on, let's have a few rolls of the dice and see if your luck holds.'

After Marcus had stumbled to bed, owing his friend almost a month's pay, Quintus sat up for a while. The drumming of his fingers on the table betrayed the unease he felt about the news Marcus had brought. Before retiring himself, he went to see his commander. He slept easier that night knowing that Petillus Cerealis had put the fort on battle alert.

***

As Marcus rode out through the gates of the fort the next morning, he passed a company of men marching off towards the amphitheatre, although it was still very early. He supposed they must be going for a drill. With the governor away, he would have expected routine to be relaxed. They were certainly pretty relaxed at the Colonia back in Camulodunum. He

couldn't remember seeing any soldiers drilling in the amphitheatre since his arrival. He had imagined army life to be
much stricter, so it was good to have his faith restored. Nice
to know Petillus Cerealis was keeping up the standard.

Once outside, he pulled his horse to a standstill. He had
been intending to stay longer, but Quintus seemed preoccupied and almost glad to see him go. He supposed he had gone
on a bit about the girl Gwenneth. He hadn't been able to help
himself. She was so lovely and holding her had filled him with
tenderness. He had stayed awake all night to make sure she
was safe. When at last there was silence in the hall, she had
fallen asleep and he had looked at her face for hours. Every
detail was imprinted on his mind, even down to the fine
golden hairs on her upper lip. More than anything, he wanted
to return to Boudicca's territory and try and to find her but it
would be hopeless. Reluctantly, he turned the horse's head to
the south and set off for Camulodunum.

He was still a few hours ride from the Colonia when he
heard the sound of running water. The sun was hot on his back
and a track leading off from the road looked cool and inviting.
It followed a small stream and was shaded by a row of alders.
It was two hours or so before sunset, and he had plenty of
provisions. On impulse, he left the road. The track seemed
well defined and with luck, would cut off a bit of the dogleg
at the end of his route. At worst, he would have to ford the
stream and hack through the wood to get back home, but the
water was shallow and the trees were widely spaced, so it
shouldn't be too hard on him or his horse.

***

Gwenneth was dangling her bare feet in the stream where
it crossed a clearing in the wood. It was good to rest. The journey here had taken all day and all night, travelling cross country. The leather of her shoes had worn thin and the cold water
numbed her bruised and blistered skin. On the bank beside her
gleamed three trout. She had caught them the way Corin had
taught her when they were children and planned to stuff them

71

with herbs and grill them for her supper but for the moment she wanted to do nothing. She had found this place that morning and realised she could take refuge here for a while. There were plenty of fish, and although it was the wrong time of the year for hedgerow fruit, she would be able to pound seed heads for porridge and use the stalks to weave rope for traps. She had made herself a shelter by cutting willow shoots and weaving them into hurdles and used turves from the bank to keep out the rain. It had been hard work and she was tired.

She lowered herself down and felt her muscles relax. The sun warmed her body and the grass stirred in the breeze, tickling her bare skin. She remembered his hands, stroking her to calm her as you would a horse or a dog, and in her dreams, she imagined it was him caressing her again, finding the sensitive place in the crook of her arm and running his fingertips down to rub the mound below her thumb.

She jerked awake. It was him. She struggled to sit up and pulled her tunic down over her knees. Her cheeks were burning.

'What are you doing here?' Her voice was curt. She was ashamed of the thoughts she had been having whilst she dozed in the grass.

He let his hand fall to his side. He had made her angry.

'I didn't mean to startle you,' he said. 'I came to drink from the stream and saw you lying on the grass. I just wanted to check you were alright.'

When he had seen her lying there at first, he had thought she was dead, and his heart had stopped beating. Then he had seen the gentle rise and fall of her breast and realised she was only sleeping. He had tethered his horse and trod carefully through the grass fearing to wake her. He wanted to look at her again. She was even more beautiful than he remembered, and he hadn't been able to resist reaching out to touch her.

'Well, I'm fine. Now you can go.'

'No, I can't leave you here alone.'

'You must. It is dangerous for us both if they find us together.'

'If who finds us together? Tell me what's going on. Why are you out here alone so far from home?'

'You wouldn't understand.'

'Try me. I want to help.'

His brown eyes were filled with such compassion that her resolve weakened. She had been trying to stay strong by taking care of the practicalities, but the thought of spending the rest of her days as an outcast suddenly overwhelmed her. She wanted to cry and fall into his arms and let him hug her and tell her everything was all right. But it wasn't. Well, maybe if he knew, he really could help her. She turned to face him.

'What do you know of the druids?'

He was bewildered. Her question seemed to have nothing to do with their situation. 'Very little other than they are a bit like our priests but I don't see.'

'Just listen,' she said impatiently. 'The druids are not like your priests. They guard the path between us and the spirit world. Their power is terrible and to cross them can mean death – or worse.'

'So, what has that got to do with you and me?'

'Don't interrupt. Just let me finish. They have a rite called the living sacrifice. It is used to cure the mortally ill. They take the blood and flesh from an enemy. The flesh taken must not be too much to cause death immediately but the victim must die eventually to bar entry to the spirit world for the one who is ill, the one the rite is meant to cure.'

'What happens to the flesh and blood,' asked Marcus. He had a dreadful suspicion he already knew and could taste bile in the back of his throat.

'It is cooked and given to the sick man to eat.'

Marcus turned away and retched.

'So, now you know,' said Gwenneth to his back as he was sick on the grass. 'You were such a victim.'

'Who was the sick man?' asked Marcus when he had recovered enough to speak.

'My uncle, Prasutagus. I saved you from death and so my uncle did not get better. He died. Because he died, his tribe has lost their autonomy, his treasure has been looted, my aunt has been flogged and my cousins have been raped.'

'None of this is your fault,' said Marcus. 'Prasutagus was an old man. The days of his autonomy were numbered. Eating human flesh is against all the laws of gods and men. You were absolutely right to help me. You should not have run away.'

'I haven't run away. I've been cast out,' said Gwenneth, her lips trembling. 'The druid saw my reaction when you came into the hall and then noticed your missing finger. Such an unusual wound and clearly recent – it didn't take him long to make the connection. Now I have nowhere to go.'

'You must have other family or friends you can stay with.'

'Don't you understand!' she cried. 'I'm cursed.'

'Nonsense. No one is going to know what happened except you and the druid.'

'Look!' She lifted her hair away from her temple and he noticed the ugly burn.

The kiss was an impulse meant to comfort her. At the touch of his lips, her first instinct was to pull away but then her body took over. This is what she had been dreaming of as she lay in the grass soaking up the warmth of the sun. His hold tightened as he felt her relax. Her mouth opened beneath his and their tongues met and twisted together. Gwenneth felt she was floating on a sea of sensation. He had loosed the shoulder clasps that held up her tunic and his hands were roaming freely over her naked breasts. Her nipples were hard as cherry stones and as his fingers brushed repeatedly over and around them, she felt a burning like ice began in her belly and spread though her thighs. She knew she should stop him but instead she pulled him down onto the grass. After all she had nothing left to lose. The druid believed them to be lovers already.

Hurriedly, Marcus unclasped his belt and pulled off his own tunic. He rolled on top of her and she guided him inside her. A momentary pain made her cry out. He started to pull away but she gripped his buttocks tightly and began to move rhythmically under him, shuddering with each thrust. The sensation of ice and fire in her limbs became more intense as Marcus moved faster on top of her. Then, suddenly, all tension was released as if she was a bowstring when the arrow is let fly. She moaned softy. Marcus plunged into her more deeply and shouted out in triumph as he felt his own release. He gently withdrew and they clung together exhausted on the damp grass.

When they woke, the light was filtering through the trees casting dappled patterns on their naked skin. They were lying side by side. Marcus turned towards her and buried his head in her hair. It gleamed in the golden light of the sun like burnished copper and smelled of honey. He pulled gently on one of the soft curls and twisted around his fingers.

'I'm sorry if I hurt you. It was the first time for me.'

Gwenneth felt as if the inside of her body was melting. She turned too and looked steadily into his eyes.

'It was my first time as well.'

They smiled at each other.

'I'm starving,' said Marcus.

Gwenneth laughed, 'Me too.'

He stood up and held out a hand to help her to her feet. He gathered up her tunic and tenderly slipped it back over her head and refastened the brooches. She went barefoot down to the river and prepared the fish whilst he donned his own tunic and collected some wood. He soon had a fire blazing and Gwenneth put the fish in the embers to roast. The familiarity of these domestic routines removed the last of the awkwardness between them, and they chatted as if had known each other forever. They shared the beer and bread Marcus had brought with him for the journey. After their meal, Marcus picked Gwenneth up and took her into the shelter. The moon was low on the eastern horizon when they finally fell asleep.

***

Gerry woke up with a start. She was not in her tent. She was in a proper bed instead of her sleeping bag. Then she remembered. She turned cautiously onto her side to look at the man sleeping next to her. Moonlight was streaming through the caravan window, and she could see every detail of his face from the long lashes casting shadows on his cheeks to the stubble that darkened his skin. What the hell had she done?

Chapter 9

It was the veterans who they hated the most because they had taken land from the Britons who thy called slaves and captives.

Tacitus. Annals 31.8-14

The Elders stood waiting in a circle around the great oak chair. The queen had summoned them to the palace. Three days had passed since the Roman army had left. Boudicca parted the hangings that curtained off the alcove and came into the hall.

'One of you has been sending reports to our enemies.' She stalked along the lines of old men and stopped in front of Anted.

'You were seen going to Barthu's hut after the Council meeting,' she said. 'Don't try to deny it. Your limp gave you away.'

'He is a kinsman. We had family business to discuss,' Anted protested.

'Strange business that made it necessary for him to leave the village immediately and take the road south although the light was fading,' said the druid from the doorway.

'Barthu has confessed,' said the queen. She walked stiffly to her great oak chair, sitting down with an exaggerated show of care. In truth, her back was healing well thanks to the druid's salve. The ostentatious display was to remind the Council of her injuries to justify her actions. She intended to exact a terrible revenge.

'I am no more a traitor than you,' said Anted defiantly.

Boudicca looked at him in surprise. She had not expected this. She recovered quickly and sprang to her feet.

'You dare to call me a traitor!' She loosened the brooch at her shoulder, crossing her arm to hide her breasts as the top of her tunic fell down to her waist. She turned away and bent her head forward. The raised welts that criss-crossed her pale skin drew a collective gasp from the old men. Boudicca's smile was hidden by her braids. It was just the reaction she wanted. She straightened up, pulling at the material and clasping the brooch securely. When she was covered, she turned back, sure that she would get her way now, but Anted had not finished.

'It is ten years since you left my son to fight the Romans alone,' he shouted. 'Then we had a chance but needed every man in our tribe on our side. You persuaded Prasutagus to stay out of it and that is how he became the king and the Emperor's puppet. Now the Romans have grown strong and we have no chance. Your pathetic attempts to hang on to power shame you and our warriors and have brought the punishment you deserve. You may now be thinking to rebel but only because you have been humiliated and robbed. It would be better for us all if you were to accept the new arrangement. You will only lead us to greater defeat. You may call me a spy, but informing the governor of your schemes was in all our interest. I would rather become a citizen of Rome than the victim of a ruthless woman.'

He turned and limped out of the palace. Boudicca was stunned by his words. How had he known she was planning rebellion? Why had he notified the Procurator of her intention to change Prasutagus' will? Had he done his own deal with Rome? She thought quickly.

'You heard his confession. He admits to betraying us to the governor. He knows of many other secrets that the Romans would find useful.' She scanned the faces in front of her. They were like sheep ready to be herded in any direction she wished. 'He must die. His body must be thrown into the bog so it leaves no trace.'

The old men hung their heads. No one dared to argue. Boudicca turned to the druid.

'Take care of it,' she commanded and he followed Anted out of the palace. She turned back to face the Council. 'Now to the future. Our warriors are ready for war. We have lost our independence – are we also to lose our lands? We must fight now before our young men are taken into slavery and all our wealth is stripped from us. Who will join me?'

Rorcus was the first to take the speaker's rod. 'My sister's husband followed Anted's son ten years ago. Now, her sons are fatherless and she gathers crops for other men's wives. I think Anted spoke well. If we could not free ourselves then, what chance have we now?'

'You speak like a coward,' said Boudicca with a sneer. 'Ten years ago, the time was wrong. Now my spies tell me that the governor is struggling to contain the Silurians and is many days march from here. The veterans in Camulodunum are old and weak and have been out of active service too long to remember how to fight. The town has no defences and is ripe for sacking. When they hear of our success, others will join us and by the time we reach Londinium, our army will be unstoppable. The tribes in the south are disillusioned by failed promises and sick of being oppressed by a corrupt empire. Once the Romans have been forced out, we will be able to defend our shores from further invasions. Send out the messengers and prepare for war.'

***

Quintus struggled to his feet. His left arm hung uselessly at his side, mangled by the wheels of the chariot that had knocked him to the ground. His head had struck a rock as he fell. A raging thirst told him he must have been unconscious for a long time. All around him lay the bodies of his fallen comrades. Nearly half a legion had been massacred in the ambush. They had caught the soldiers as they came over the hill and thrown them into confusion with a chariot rush. The land either side of the road was thickly wooded, and when the men had tried to escape from the path of the galloping horses, they had been cut down by the natives waiting amongst the trees.

He tried to walk but fell to the ground again as his legs collapsed from under him. There was only one thought in his head, to get to Camulodunum and warn of the approaching hordes. Somehow, he dragged his bruised body from the bank onto the road. Crawling with his one good arm, he began to inch his way south.

***

Boudicca swept through the deserted streets in her painted chariot with Mardunad and Valda crouching at her feet. Behind her came the massed ranks of the allied tribes making their way to the temple of Claudius, where the citizens had taken refuge with the shattered remnants of the Roman troops. The warriors of the Iceni and Trinovantes stormed through the colonnaded porticos seeking an entrance. The marble was impenetrable. Undeterred, they pounded the doors, but they were lined with metal and could not be broken. For two days, they attacked the walls with anything that they could find. At last, the stone was breached. The people left inside fought to the last but in the end, no one was left to resist. No prisoners were taken in the sacking of the Colonia. Fires raged day and night through the streets of wooden buildings and the air was filled with the stench of burning flesh. The rebels finally withdrew to the native settlement to celebrate their victory. Hundreds of farm animals were slaughtered to feed the native army and camp followers.

Boudicca gloated as she watched the dancing that followed the feast. She had revelled in the orgy of death and destruction. After her humiliation at the hands of the Romans, the Iceni and Trinovantes had rallied to her summons. They had ambushed the Ninth legion on its way to strengthen the defences of Camulodunum and not a soul had survived. Then, they had marched on the town itself and utterly destroyed it. But this was only the beginning. She would make Catus Decianus pay. Londinium would be next.

***

Marcus was trying to make Gwenneth understand. He knelt in front of her as she sat with her back against a tree. 'Don't you see I have to leave? If I stay any longer, I will be executed for desertion.'

'You told me yourself that discipline was lax with the governor away. They won't even have noticed your absence. You could say you had to go to Londinium to report to Decianus. You don't have to go at all. You're just tired of me already.'

He took her hands from her lap and stroked the inside of her wrists with his thumbs. 'Sweetheart, I won't be gone long. I just have to see what has been happening and if there are any messages from Paulinus.'

She batted his hands away, not wanting to be coaxed or petted.

'You just want to go and have a laugh with your friends and boast about how easy it is to seduce the native girls in the woods. Well, go then, but don't expect me to wait for you to come back.' She hung her head and her hair fell forward hiding her face so he couldn't see the unshed tears that were blinding her.

Marcus could feel his temper rising. Why was she being so obstinate? He took her under the chin and tipped her face so she was forced to look at him. When he saw that she was crying, he was immediately contrite. He gently wiped away a tear that had spilled onto her cheek.

'Gwenneth, don't do this. These last few days have been the best of my life. I feel like I have known you forever. I want to stay more than anything in the world, but I cannot abandon my duties. It would break my mother's heart if I brought disgrace on the family. If I go back now, I can ask for official leave. I am sure it would be granted, as there is nothing that can possibly require my attendance. I swear on all I believe in that I will find a way for us to stay together always. I love you, my darling.'

With these words, he took her into his arms and her resistance melted. They clung together for a long time. He released her at last and she leant back against the tree.

'When will you go?'

'Early tomorrow.'

'So, we have one more night?'

'No,' he protested. 'We will have thousands of nights.' He bent his head to kiss her. She resisted at first. She had a strong sense of foreboding and wished he did not feel honour-bound to go. But he was insistent and her lips parted in surrender to his will.

That night, there was a poignant quality to their love-making. They joined together many times through the short summer night. They would barely have recovered their breath when it would begin again. As they lay panting, Gwenneth would run her fingers over his chest, tracing the swell of the muscles, trying to imprint the feel of his skin on her memory. Intermittently, they talked. The moonlight winked through the wicker walls of their home and cast eerie shadows on their sprawled limbs. He told her of his childhood in the sun-drenched fields of his father's estate. For him, life had always been secure and easy. His career had been mapped out for him since he was a small boy. In turn, she tried to explain to him what it was like growing up in the uncertain years after the conquest and the pain of losing her mother and father and growing up in Boudicca's household. They carefully avoided talking about the recent past. Their experiences were still too raw.

Towards morning, he woke to find her lying close beside him, belly to belly, breast to breast. He studied her face with passionate intensity and watched her eyelids flickering in the last moments of her dreams. She smiled when her eyes finally opened and saw the way he was looking at her. He stroked the curves of her buttocks and gently lifted her to sit astride him. They moved together, slowly at first, and then more urgently, until they came together in a storm of ice and fire.

Marcus left much later than he had intended. Gwenneth insisted on catching a fish for breakfast, but she was clumsy and he paced the riverbank for nearly an hour until she triumphantly pulled a trout out of the water. Then his horse refused to be caught and shied skittishly every time he approached her.

He was close to losing his temper when she suddenly suc-
cumbed and allowed him to put on her bridle. He was just
about to mount when Gwenneth told him to wait whilst she
fetched bread and beer for him to take on his journey. He
ground his teeth in frustration as he waited for her to return.
She came back out of breath and empty-handed having
searched everywhere before she remembered they had eaten
all the rations he brought with him the day before. He gave
her a perfunctory kiss on the cheek and leapt into the saddle
before she could think of anything else to keep him there.

He had not gone more than a hundred yards before he was
sorry for his abrupt departure. He considered going back to
say good-bye but thought better of it. He would probably find
her crying and he would have to stay and comfort her. After
all, he would not be gone long. Best to get it over with now
that he had started. By the time he reached the road, he was
whistling. He wondered what had happened whilst he had
been away.

Gwenneth watched until he was out of sight. She knew
she had been silly making excuses to keep him with her a little
longer. It had just irritated him. But she was so afraid he would
forget her as soon as he was amongst his own people again.
The sound of him whistling made her sure of it. She sat down
on the bank and twisted her fingers in the grass. She didn't
know how to fill the empty hours until he came back – if he
ever did.

Chapter 10

Due to the activities of rebel spies the citizens were unpre-
pared. They neither built defensive ditches and ramparts nor
arranged for women and the elderly to leave, relying only on
the temple for protection as if the country was at peace. So
they were overwhelmed by the first attack of the barbarian
hordes and everywhere except the temple was pillaged or
burned to the ground. Those that survived took refuge in the
temple but after 2 days siege even that refuge was lost.
Tacitus. Annals 32.7-12

Smoke hung like a pall in the still air. Marcus dismounted and
looked out over the remains of the Colonia. Not one building
had been left standing. It was hard to equate this devastation
with the thriving town he had left only days ago. Choking on
the acrid fumes, he led his horse through the rubble. Here and
there, amongst the smouldering heaps of wood, he saw the
blackened and charred limbs of people who had lived and
worked and then died in the new town.

A child's hoop lay in the gutter. Beside it was a little body
with the stomach torn open and the guts spilling out onto the
cobbles. Disaster seems to have struck without warning. The
contents of the shops lay where they had fallen when the
shelving supports collapsed. Nothing seemed to have been
looted or salvaged. He wondered at the nature of the attack
and who had come in such numbers to cause such utter ruin.

He did not wonder for long. The answer came to him as
he stood in front of the ruins of the temple. This must be the
rebellion Quintus had predicted. Now he felt ashamed of what
he had said that night at the inn, not so long ago. If this was
action, he didn't want any of it. War was not noble, it was ugly.

His face burned at his idealism. What a fool Quintus must have thought him.

Thinking of his friend jolted him into action. Whatever had happened here must not be repeated. He would ride at once to Durobrivae and warn Cerialis. The Ninth legion could stop this. He picked his way carefully through the wreckage and the broken bodies. When he reached the road, he threw himself back into the saddle. At his urging, the horse broke into a gallop, and they thundered off back the way they had come.

After an hour of hard riding, Marcus pulled his horse up to rest. They had just crested a hill and his attention was caught by a movement on the road below. He shielded his eyes against the glare of the sun on the limestone surface. In the dark shadow cast by the trees that lined the road, he saw the glint of metal. He gathered the reins in his left hand and drew his sword in readiness. The mare responded to the light pressure of his knees against her flanks and moved slowly down the slope. As he drew closer and his eyes adjusted, he realised that the glint came from the edge of cuirass. The Roman soldier it belonged to was a crumpled figure beneath a coating of white dust. At the sound of an approaching horse, the figure raised his head, which seemed to be caked in red mud. Marcus was shocked to find himself looking into a pair of familiar brown eyes.

'Quintus,' he cried out in disbelief. He swung hastily down from his horse, letting his sword fall with a clang to the ground as he reached for the water bottle and rushed over to his friend's side. It was not mud but blood, he saw with horror, still oozing from the matted hair at his friend's temples. He knelt down and took the wounded man in his arms, supporting his head whilst Quintus gulped from the leather flask. His hand sank into the mangled flesh that had once been an arm. He stifled a cry. Quintus clearly had no feeling left on that side as he gave no sign the arm hurt him.

'What in Hades happened to you,' said Marcus when Quintus feebly pushed away the water bottle to show he had drunk enough.

'Ambush. Iceni. Legion. Massacred. Camulodunum in danger. No time. Go now. Swear. No time go.' He became more and more agitated. His breath came in great gasps. 'You go. Swear.'

Marcus realised his friend was dying. There was no sign of any ambush here. Quintus must have crawled many miles down this road in a desperate attempt to send warning to Camulodunum. It was too late for that now, but he could still warn the governor.

'I will go. I swear.'

Quintus slumped back into the arms that held him. His eyes began to glaze over. Within moments, he was dead. Marcus dragged the body further into the forest. He didn't have either the time or the tools to mourn or dig a grave but had to protect the body from chance discovery as best as he could and away from wolves and scavengers. He thrust it deep into a thicket of brambles using his cloak to protect his arms from the sharp thorns. It would have to do. He couldn't stay any longer. He made a vow to return soon and collect whatever remained of his friend for an honourable burial.

His horse had found some grass beside the road but came at once to his whistle. He put his arms around her neck and buried his face in her soft mane, drawing comfort from her solid presence. He wanted to go back to Gwenneth. In the warmth of her body, he could forget what he had seen. It would only mean a short delay, perhaps an hour at most.

Then he remembered the scene earlier in the day. She might trick him into staying longer. After all, the message he had for the governor would have a direct effect on her people. She felt guilty enough already. It would be better if she knew nothing about it until it was all over. He had the map of the main roads Quintus had given him and could find his way without a guide. With luck, he would be back in four or five days, and she wasn't expecting him for two or three days at least. He put his desires to one side. He was bound by his oath and by his duty to his fallen comrades. Duty must come before love. He leaped on the mare's back and gave her the signal to move off. At the top of the rise, he raised his hand in salute to his friend before plunging down into the next dip of the road.

Marcus reached the first staging post as dusk was falling. It lay at the junction where his own road west crossed the broad highway that led north to Durobrivae. The fortress would be deserted. A whole legion fallen to the rebels. Quintus appeared to be the sole survivor. What strength he had to drag himself so far when so terribly wounded. The boy's will be hardened. He would be a worthy successor. He would get the message through to the governor and save the province from disaster even if he had to ride night and day.

The clatter of hooves on the cobbles brought the guard rushing out into the courtyard. He was eager for news, as there hadn't been any traffic for the last couple of days. A few words from Marcus and the lull was explained. He quickly grasped the urgency and shouted to the stable hand to saddle a horse whilst he scurried off to the kitchen in search of refreshments and provisions for the boy's journey.

Within the hour, Marcus was astride a new mount after gulping down a mug of beer and a meat pie. He had more pies in his saddlebag wrapped in vine leaves, which reminded him of home.

He wondered what was happening there and felt a sudden longing to see his family. He thought of his mother. When he had left home, she had reminded him that he must always do his duty, whatever the cost. Well, he would make her proud.

His water flask had been refilled and the innkeeper had given him advice on the best route which was now marked on the map that Quintus had given him when they parted back at Durobrivae. How long ago that seemed. Now his friend was dead, butchered by that evil woman and her people. He berated himself for once feeling pity for Boudicca and her daughters.

The stable hand released the bridle and the gelding was off like a javelin in flight, eager for exercise after being cooped up in the stable. At first, Marcus let the horse have his head and the milestones flashed by, but then he slowed their pace to a steady canter. They had a long way to go, and he didn't want to test the horse's stamina just yet.

It was after midnight when he reached the inn that stood at the next staging post. It had been locked up for the night, and Marcus had to hammer at the wooden door for some time before a face appeared at one of the upstairs windows. It took a while before Marcus could make the innkeeper aware of the urgency of his business. At last, he heard the noise of bolts being drawn, and a figure came out of the door holding a candle aloft. He turned out to be Trinovantes but seemed to be as worried as Marcus about a revolt. Perhaps the revolt was localised after all, thought Marcus. Maybe he should have travelled on to the fort at Durobrivae to check. No, Quintus had been adamant. Anyway, there was no time to lose. His gelding had been replaced with a sturdy mountain pony whilst he was eating one of the pies and drinking the last of his water. The innkeeper went off to refill his water bottle, and Marcus got acquainted with his new mount. He hoped she would be strong enough to carry him for the rest of the journey, as he was approaching hostile territory and unlikely to get another.

The pony felt strange compared with the finely bred animals used by the army. It did not respond well to his signals and Marcus had to kick her hard to get her to leave the yard. As he left, he heard the bolts on the gates being hammered home. After seeing the wreckage at Camulodunum, Marcus doubted the gates would be much defence against the hordes that were even now probably rampaging through the province. The night air was cold. He gave the pony another kick and huddled in his cloak as it settled into a rhythmic trot. The steady drumming of hooves was soporific, and he drifted into the twilight zone between sleeping and waking. The experience of years kept him upright on the broad back whilst his mind wandered between past, present and future.

The sky gradually lightened as day dawned. Marcus was riding through a wooded valley. A thick mist rolled through the trees and swirled about the pony's knees. As he descended towards the valley floor, Marcus could see no more than a few feet ahead and had to trust his pony to find the way down to the river he had seen in the distance. He could hear water running over the rocky path then suddenly his pony was in it. The current was strong and he could sense the pony struggling to keep its footing. As they reached the opposite bank, the mist began to clear.

That ford was the first of many. By midday, they had struggled through seven streams. When they stopped to rest, the pony's flanks were heaving with exhaustion and Marcus' thighs were raw where his wet skin had been chafed by the leather saddle. He didn't dare dismount in case he couldn't get back on again. He let the pony graze whilst he drank from his flask and ate the last of his pies. He reckoned he had another twenty miles to ride to the fort at Deva, where he would find the governor. From his map, he had seen it lay on the estuary of the river the road now followed. He should be there by early evening. He pulled on the reins and the pony reluctantly raised its head from the succulent grass. One hard kick and they were once again trotting at the steady pace which had brought them nearly seventy miles.

***

'So, Marcus Valerius Saturninus, you finally join my staff.' Paulinus stretched out his legs beneath the desk and leaned back in his chair to study the young man who had just entered. Marcus flushed. This was not quite how he had envisaged their first meeting. Throughout the long and difficult journey, he had been imagining the way he would be greeted as a hero with a flattering speech of welcome praising his courage and endurance and the way he had put his duty to his country above everything else – even love, although he would keep that part of it to himself. Instead, he found a messenger had already arrived with the news of the uprising and had presented accurate and first-hand knowledge.

He learned that only half the Ninth had been marching to the aid of the veterans in the Colonia at Camulodunum. The rest of the men had been transferred from Lindum to Durobrivae where they were ready to deal with any rebels who ventured north. Cerealis had been able to act quickly because of the report he had from Quintus on the treatment of Boudicca and her daughters. Although the ambush had foiled his attempt to protect the Colonia, Cerealis had escaped with his cavalry and sent a message to the governor. Paulinus had already sent orders for the second to march up from Isca and meet the rest of the Ninth who would be coming down south. The plan was for the two legions to intercept the rebels to the west of Londinium.

It was all well in hand, thought Marcus, as he stood in front of the governor like a naughty schoolboy. There had been no need for him to come at all. He could have been back with Gwenneth by now if he had carried on to Durobrivae and found out the real state of events. With hindsight it was obvious Quintus was delirious. And there was no trace of any fighting close by. He had wanted to prove himself a man and instead, had made himself look foolish and reckless to his superiors and had been cruel and faithless to his lover.

Paulinus was waiting for him to speak. He raised his eyes from the floor and found the governor smiling him.

'You have not done so badly,' he said. In fact, some of my commanders could not have done as well, despite their greater experience here. You have managed to get yourself across some pretty difficult countryside, even though you have not been long here in the province. Very brave, if a little hasty. Anyway, now you are here, we can make some use of you. Take a look at this.'

Marcus went to join him on the other side of the desk on which a map was spread out. He had hoped he would be sent back east. Paulinus was explaining something. He dragged his thoughts away from Gwenneth and started to listen. As he grasped what the governor was saying, his disappointment vanished.

An attack was to be mounted on the large island of Mona at the north-eastern tip of the Silurian territory. It was where the Druidic cult sprang from and the centre of resistance in the west so it had been the target of successive generals since Claudius had declared the province part of the Empire. Until now, the army had not been in a position to attack but Paulinus had finally subdued the rest of Siluria after two hard-fought campaigns. Mona was now almost within reach. This was the reason he had not immediately marched east on receiving news of the rebellion. He was confident that Cerealis could deal with Boudicca and her followers. Two legions of Roman soldiers could easily take care of a native rabble. The fact that half a legion had gone had not changed his mind. Once the Druids were wiped out, the resistance would crumble.

'How will you get across the straits?' asked Marcus, studying the map.

'We have spent the winter constructing a fleet of flat-bottomed boats,' said Paulinus. 'That's why I chose this location on the estuary for my headquarters. Now we are ready. The infantry left last week to take up this position.' He pointed at the map. 'It's just opposite the place I have chosen to land. Tomorrow, I leave with the cavalry to join them. You will travel with me as messenger. It will be a good experience for you. The officer outside will find you a billet. Get a good night's sleep. You'll need all your wits about you tomorrow.'

Marcus left, his mind reeling. He wanted to be part of the military action. It was something he had dreamed of since he was a small boy, and so when two years ago, back in Rome, Paulinus had suggested to Marcus' father that his son should join his staff, the young man had begged his father to agree. They had been dining together in Rome. Marcus had been allowed to eat with the two old friends and listened openmouthed as they reminisced about the time they had fought together in Mauritania. Paulinus had spoken casually about his new appointment in Britannia and said it was a good place for the son of a Roman senator to start his career. Marcus' father had said he was too young, but Paulinus had remembered the boy's enthusiasm when one of his personal staff had fallen ill. It was unusual for a boy of only seventeen to travel so far from home, but because Paulinus was a close friend, Marcus had finally been allowed to go. Now with a battle in the offing, Marcus was confused to find himself longing to be with a woman, a woman he had left to go on a fool's errand to please a dying man raving in the delirium of a raging fever. It was some comfort to know that, actually, now he had no choice. The dice had been thrown, and he would have to stay here with the governor until Paulinus had achieved his objective and crushed this final pocket of resistance.

The officer detailed to take care of him took Marcus to the store, where the quartermaster kitted him out with woollen trousers, a shirt, a leather jerkin and a new red cloak to replace his own clothes, which were wet and filthy from the long journey. He was also given a short sword and a shield. The officer then showed the boy to the dormitory. It was empty, but he could hear laughter from the mess hall. He wondered how the soldiers could be so relaxed with a battle pending and thought he would not be able to sleep. The bed was hard, but he was exhausted from the two days he had spent in the saddle and did not wake until morning.

Chapter 11

So he made preparations to attack the island of Mona by constructing a fleet of flat-bottomed boats to negotiate the shallow and unpredictable waters of the channel to transport the infantry. The cavalry followed by swimming at the side of their horses.

Tacitus Annals 29.8 – 29.11

Gerry squatted on the ground and concentrated on the hard clay surface she was trowelling. She had left Peter sleeping and gone back to her own tent before dawn. What on earth had possessed her to go to his caravan last night, she thought. Too much to drink, and all her good intentions had flown out the window. Worse still, their lovemaking, if you could call it that, was disastrous. She was still undecided about the wisdom of sleeping with him and couldn't relax properly. He had tried to come inside her but much too soon, and she wasn't ready. Then he went soft and nothing she had done had any effect – except to reveal that she had rather more experience than she wanted him to know about. In the end, he had turned over and pretended to sleep. To save her dignity, she had done the same until she could tell by his breathing that he really was. She wondered how she was going to face him now. He hadn't appeared on site yet, which was unusual. Then she heard him come out of the caravan and kept her head down.

'Tom, I'm going with Anthony up to Warham Camp to do some dowsing. We won't be back until late this evening. I'm leaving you in charge. Any problems, send me a text if you can get a signal. If not, ring me from the hostel.'

'No problem, boss. Good luck.'

Well, that gives me some breathing space, thought Gerry. She realised she had stopped working while the two men were talking and bent, once more, over the job she had been given to do by Tom. The site was now at an interesting stage. The rubble that had appeared once they had taken off the turf had been scraped clean of any top soil and drawn and photographed by Tom. Then, everyone had worked together removing the tumbled stones to reveal what was, unmistakeably, the four walls of a room in a substantial building. In the process, they had found a lot of animal bones and featureless grey pottery. There had been a later Roman settlement in the area to the west of where they were excavating this season, and Peter had come to the conclusion that what they had found so far was probably material from the rubbish dumps associated with that settlement, which had been spread on the fields that surrounded that town after the site they were working on had been abandoned. He was still convinced that the building itself was much earlier.

Inside the walls, under the rubble, there were layers of white chalky material which had in turn been drawn, photographed and removed. Peter had identified these as floors but frustratingly, they seemed to have been regularly cleaned in the time when the building was in use and so far, nothing had been found which could help with dating. Unfortunately, the trench only included this one room. The rest of the villa, if that was what it was, disappeared under the baulk. Peter was already talking about another excavation season next year.

That was one of Peter's strengths as an excavation director, Gerry thought as she trowelled – that he shared his thoughts with the rest of the team. Every morning as soon as the volunteers had straggled in from the hostel, he would assemble them at the edge of the trench and point out the features that had been revealed the previous day and what they might mean. The briefings were fairly short but it was a great way to motivate the team, and Gerry had noticed that everyone went to collect their tools for the day with a new sense of purpose when he had finished speaking.

They all started off with a bucket, hand shovel and trowel, but the young men and women took turns to do the harder manual work. This was taking the excavated material to the spoil heap after it had been scraped from the ground with trowels, scooped into the hand shovel, transferred into buckets and emptied into the line of wheelbarrows along the side of the trench. The American students were all looking much fitter as a result of this routine but still seemed to be having trouble getting up in the morning!

Now, at the start of the second week, Tom had decided they were ready to begin looking at what was happening outside the building. He had asked Gerry to carefully scrape the hard clay surface next to the walls to try and find the edges of a construction trench. She worked quietly and methodically throughout the morning, and when Tom called a halt for lunch, she had trowelled the entire area between the edge of the wall and the side of the trench. She was just scooping up the last few crumbs when Tom came over.

'Great job, Gerry,' he said. 'The edge of the construction trench is showing up really well.'

Gerry stood up, scraping the last bit of earth from her trowel onto the shovel. She was thrilled to see that there was a clear distinction between the brown clay that covered most of the ground where she was working and a thin strip of darker looser soil immediately adjacent to the limestone blocks that edged the wall. She had noticed there was a slight change in texture as she trowelled but had been so absorbed in what she was doing that she hadn't realised the difference showed up visually.

'You can draw that this afternoon then we might take a section through to see exactly what's happening. There seems to be a bit of a bulge here near the corner.'

Gerry was still recovering from the surprise at being asked to do the drawing and it was a minute or two before she looked at where Tom was pointing. She saw there was a circle of lighter material that looked like a small pit. Something hovered at the edge of her memory. Wasn't there some sort of ritual connected with building foundations in the Roman period?

She cast her mind back to the lectures she had sat through in Bristol. It remained stubbornly blank. Not surprising considering what was happening at the time.

She picked up the bucket and stepped up out onto the grass, taking care not to stand on the edge of the trench. Only rookies did that. The side of the trench acted as a visual record of the layers that had been excavated which would be drawn at the end of the dig and she didn't want the embarrassment of it collapsing beforehand and all that vital information being lost.

It didn't take Gerry long to draw the plan of the area she had trowelled. She had done quite a lot of archaeological drawing on the university training excavation and had been hoping she would have a chance to use her skills here. She traced the wall from another plan to save time, and then it was just a question of accurately plotting the points along its line where the soil changed colour and texture.

When she had finished, Tom took some photographs and set up a string across the darker soil by the corner of the wall so she could excavate half the feature leaving a section, which could be drawn before the other half was removed.

Gerry carefully probed the darkest soil with her trowel and found it was much finer than the rest of the construction trench and was obviously lying on top of it. She scraped the edge. A small yellow disc appeared just below the surface. The sound and feel of the trowel as it met the disc was unmistakeable. Not pottery, not stone, but bone. Suddenly, her memory of that lecture came flooding back. Neo-natals – still born babies – that was what the Romans buried in the foundations of their villas.

'Tom!' Something in her voice made him stop what he was doing and come over immediately. She gestured with her trowel at the disc in the ground. Her hand was shaking. 'I think it's a baby's skull.'

Tom jumped into the trench and squatted beside her, taking his own trowel from his back pocket. He prodded gently, revealing a little more of the curved surface. Their eyes met.

'I think you might be right,' he said. Then he noticed the look on her face. 'It's OK. You did the right thing. We will need to expose a little bit more though to check if it's human. Once you've done that, and our suspicions are confirmed, I'll phone Peter. He'll need to go back to the office and sort out the paperwork for the coroner.'

She stood up abruptly. 'I'm really sorry, Tom. I can't.'

She could see he was confused. Finding human remains was part and parcel of being an archaeologist. She hoped he would think there was a religious reason for her reluctance to continue. She was too upset to explain right now. She backed away and climbed awkwardly up onto the baulk, her vision clouded with unshed tears. She stumbled over to the mess caravan and sat down on the wooden bench outside. Ten minutes later, Tom joined her.

'I've seen enough to be sure now and covered everything up. I'm going down to the village to use the phone in the hostel. Will you be OK?'

She shook her head. 'Look, it would take too long to explain, but I can't stay on the site right now. Can I come with you? I want to see if I can get a room for tonight.'

She could see he was totally confused and finding her emotional response to what should be a pretty straightforward situation on an excavation difficult to deal with. He glanced in the direction of the marquee where Annie was standing in the sunshine washing pottery with a couple of the volunteers. Gerry guessed he was thinking about calling Annie over. She reached out her hand and touched his wrist.

'I don't want to talk to anyone. I just need to leave.'

'OK.' he said. 'Put your tools away and collect what you need from your tent. I'll just go and tell Annie about the discovery and explain where I'm going. With you and me gone and Peter and Anthony up at Warham, she is the next in command. What reason shall I give for you going with me?'

'Tell her I just received some bad news and need to spend some time on my own.'

'That's not going to wash – there's no signal here.'

'Tell her anything you like – make something up.' The snappy tone in her voice silenced him, and he left her to go and tell Annie they were leaving site.

She emptied her bucket on the spoil heap and took her tools back to the shed. It only took a few minutes to collect what she needed for the night and zip up her tent, but when she got to the Land Rover, Tom was already inside. He started the engine, and they drove, without speaking, down the track to the village.

Chapter 12

The enemy stood on the beach opposite. There were ranks of armed men and disorderly groups of women running amongst them brandishing torches, dressed in funerary black, hair wild like furies. Around them circled the druids, hands raised as they called on their gods. The sight was so alien to anything the Roman soldiers had ever seen that they stopped dead as if paralysed and did not even try to protect their bodies from injury as the enemy attacked. Then shamed by their general and comrades at flinching from females and fanatics, they raised the eagle and charged. All who met them were cut down and the enemy was consumed by their own flames.

Tacitus. Annals 31.1-6

It took the whole of the next day for the cavalry to reach the place chosen for the crossing to Mona. The first half of their route lay within the territory of the Deceangli, a tribe that Paulinus had defeated the previous year. As the troop crossed into the land of the Ordivici, the order went out to close ranks. The Ordivici depended on the island for their grain, so had most to lose if it was captured, so were likely to be waiting somewhere along the route or shadowing the column looking for an opportunity to attack. The expected ambush didn't materialise; and Marcus pitched his tent that night within the shelter of the earthen ramparts thrown up by the infantry whilst they waited the arrival of the governor.

At dawn, the infantry embarked and the boats were launched into the shallow waters of the straits. The cavalry plunged in behind. As the waters rose around them, the riders slipped off their horses to swim alongside, struggling to keep afloat in the fierce undertow. Marcus was grateful for the strength of his mountain pony. He twisted his fingers into her coarse mane and let himself go limp so she could drag him against the current. Even she was becoming exhausted when he felt the firm sand beneath his feet and stood up gasping for breath. His eyes were stinging from the salty water and he could barely see. He rubbed them impatiently to clear his vision and noticed a phalanx was forming nearby.

He was just about to join the formation when an inhuman sound filled the air. Hordes of black figures rushed onto the beach, wailing in chorus, hair streaming behind them, brandishing torches. Their faces were an unearthly green. Marcus, when recalling the onslaught later, would say it was as if the furies had erupted from the underworld.

The soldiers, to a man, were paralysed with fear. Nothing in their training had prepared them for this. The phalanx fragmented as they scattered, many of them retreating back into the waves and colliding with the men who were still arriving. They made an easy target for the blue-painted warriors that were next to burst out from the woods. Blood stained the water, as bodies were rolled in the surf on the incoming tide.

Then, behind the tribesmen, Marcus saw a line of druids advancing, unmistakeable in their grey-white robes. He looked down at his hand, at the place where his finger had been severed. Rage filled him and he forgot his fear. The standard-bearer had fallen not far away from him. He waded through the water and tore the Eagle from his grasp. Then he threw himself onto his pony and charged towards the advancing line of spears.

The raising of the standard gave fresh heart to the Romans. They pressed forward, yelling as they fell in behind their totem. The women, for it was only women they had mistaken for demons, were caught between the two sides. As they were pressed closer and closer together, the stench of burning mingled with the smell of blood as the torches fed on hair, clothes and flesh. The shrill screams of pain proved the wraiths to be only too human. Encouraged by their officers, the Roman soldiers regained the initiative and marched in formation through the opposing ranks. The native warriors were no match for their disciplined attack and were cut down or fled. By the time night fell, all resistance had gone and the island belonged to Rome.

* * *

The following day, Marcus was summoned to the governor's tent.

'Yesterday, you exceeded even my expectations,' said Paulinus. 'I knew your father to be brave in battle and I hoped you would take after him. You showed no fear in confronting those fanatics and helped us turn defeat into victory.'

Marcus felt a fraud as he stood in front of the governor. He started to speak, wanting to explain that he had been driven by anger not courage, but Paulinus silenced him with a gesture of dismissal. The governor had more important things on his mind. A succession of officers was reporting to get their orders for the day, and Marcus left the tent. He was standing outside wondering what to do with himself when the thundering of hooves heralded the arrival of a horseman at speed. Marcus jumped out of the way as the rider drew to a standstill in a cloud of dust, calling for the governor.

'This way,' said Marcus, flinging open the tent flap.

Paulinus looked up, frowning at the intrusion, 'What in Jupiter's name…'

The messenger pushed past Marcus and the governor's face reddened in fury.

'Secundus, what are you doing back here? I ordered you to march with the Second to Londinium.'

'I'm sorry, sir. I took your orders to Isca, but the commander was absent and had left Poenius Postumus in charge. Postumus said he didn't have the authority to dispatch the legion.'

Paulinus's face turned purple. 'Insolent fool. He will pay for his disobedience. Marcus, fetch the officers to my tent. Tomorrow, we ride to Londinium.'

***

Marcus felt as if he had spent a lifetime on a horse. His muscles ached from the effort of keeping his legs steady against the slippery leather of the saddle. He was unaccustomed to wearing the trousers he had been issued. The rough woollen material was rubbing the skin on the inside of his thighs which was already raw after the long ride he had made to Deva and then to Mona. He was riding with Paulinus and the cavalry. The governor had realised that in the time it would take for his infantry to march to Londinium, the province might be lost so he was pushing ahead to join the remnants of the Ninth. He had sent an urgent message to Postumus to mobilise the Second on pain of death.

It was a bold plan, thought Marcus. It was only a hunch that Londinium would be Boudicca's next target. She could have instead come west to join up with the insurgents in Siluria. So far, though, they had met no opposition, so it looked as if the Ordivici may have gone to join the rebel forces.

The order came to halt. The river they had reached was wide enough to carry sea-going vessels, even this far inland. The wooden bridge was only wide enough to cross in pairs. Whilst waiting his turn, Marcus had time to study the surrounding merchants' quarters. So, this was now the commercial heart of the province.

As the troop made its way to the streets, people came rushing out to greet them and the clatter of hooves on the cobbles was almost drowned out by loud cheers. Women threw flowers and blew kisses. But when the troop of horsemen passed and the crowds saw there were no infantry behind, they grew silent and turned back to their businesses and homes.

At the Procurator's residence, there was not a trace of Decianus. A messenger Paulinus had sent to the barracks returned to say they too were deserted. The governor turned to Marcus, who had followed him into the reception area.

'We cannot defend the town without reinforcements. There is no alternative but to withdraw and wait for the arrival of the infantry.'

102

'Where will you wait?' Marcus asked.

'There is a suitable place to fight just outside Verulamium,' Paulinus replied. 'We will set up a temporary camp and wait there until the Second and Fourteenth arrive.'

'And if the rebels arrive first?'

'Then we may have to sacrifice that town as well as Londinium. All the male citizens who can march must come with us now.'

'What about the women and children, sir?'

'They will have to take their chances here,' said Paulinus impatiently.

'But everyone left will be killed,' Marcus protested. 'The buildings will be razed to the ground. I saw it myself at Camulodunum.'

'I have no choice. My responsibility is to the province.'

'What about trying to evacuate them?'

'You can try if you like.'

'But I don't know how,' said Marcus hopelessly.

The governor took pity on him. 'Here, take my ring. You have my authority to use any of Decianus' staff that remain. Go through the streets, the people are probably already packing after seeing how few men I have with me, and it will be worse as they see us leave and start to panic. Try to keep some order and join me as soon as you can.'

Marcus was dismissed. He spent the rest of the day in a flurry of activity. The few men left behind, after Decianus had fled to Gaul, were surly and uncooperative, but Marcus was glad to find Lemnus and Epillicus had gone with their master. When word got out that there was, once again, a Roman presence in London, a stream of merchants presented themselves at the headquarters. They all received the same advice: leave or die. By nightfall, Marcus was hoarse from shouting above the general din.

The next day was worse. Dusk was falling as Marcus followed the last of the refugees wending their way over the bridge out of town. When he reached the high ground, he turned for a last glimpse of the town, which lay defenceless in the flood plain, an easy target for the approaching rebels.

Chapter 13

The same disaster was repeated at Verulamium. The natives, wanting only to pillage and too lazy to fight avoided the forts and garrison-posts and went instead to the place where the opportunity for plunder was greatest and least defended.
Tacitus. Annals 33.8-10

Boudicca laughed as she watched Verulamium burn. Her chariot was perched on a hill above the town. Even at this distance, she could feel the heat from the fire that engulfed the wooden buildings. She imagined the people trapped inside choking for breath and screaming in pain as their flesh shrivelled in the flames. Her hatred had grown day by day as it fed on the death and destruction she left behind her. She looked down at her daughters cringing in fear at her feet, sickened by the carnage they had witnessed and frightened by the madness in their mother's eyes.

'See the price the Romans pay for the way they treated us. Warm yourselves at the pyre of their ambitions. Fill your lungs with the smoke of their disappearing dreams. We have shown them we will not be their slaves. Like a whipped dog, their commander has run away to hide. Soon, we will flush him out and drive him and the rabble army he leads away from our shores.'

Valda had had enough. She sprang to her feet, rocking the flimsy vehicle.

'You fool yourself. We haven't yet faced the legions in battle. Your ambush took down only a fraction of their force, and the men and women you have killed could have been our allies. If you want to drive the Romans from our land, why do attack their undefended towns instead of their legions and garrisons? If they were so hateful to you, why did you collaborate in the systematic subjugation of our people? You only talk of freedom because your own power and wealth has been threatened. I hate you and what you have done. No one would have known of our shame if you had not used it as an excuse to mobilise resentment to fight your private war. It must stop. It is not too late to surrender. The governor will be merciful when he hears of the outrages committed on us by Decianus' slaves.'

Boudicca looked at her daughter with contempt. 'You are not my daughter. Milk runs in your veins, not the blood of the Icenians. Of course, it is too late. A great battle is coming. Soon, we will meet the combined forces of the remaining legions to decide who rules this kingdom.'

'Then let me and Mardunad go to find a safe place to hide. You don't need us anymore.'

'Don't you understand?' Boudicca shouted at her daughter. 'There is no safe place left for us until the Romans have been defeated. Until then, I shall keep you by my side.'

She lashed the horses and they reared in alarm. Valda lost her balance and fell back onto Mardunad. The sisters clung to each other as the chariot sped off down the slope.

***

It was lucky the hostel had an empty single room, thought Gerry. It was more expensive than she could really afford and she had to use her credit card. Hopefully, by the time the bill came through, she would have the funds to cover it in her bank account. Peter had already told her he was so pleased with the work she was doing; he would pay her the minimum hourly rate but it would take a couple of weeks to set up. She hoped their fumbling lovemaking had not changed his mind.

Lying on the bed that evening, she attempted to read, but the words paraded past on the printed page without meaning. She threw the book on the floor in despair and tried to empty her mind, but her thoughts refused to be silenced. She gave up the struggle and allowed herself to travel back in time to that awful morning just over two years ago. Deep in the past, she didn't at first hear the knock on the door.

'Gerry, are you alright?'

Peter's voice brought her back to the present with a jolt. He knocked again, louder this time.

'Gerry, let me in. I need to speak to you.'

She didn't answer and held her breath as if he could hear her breathing on the other side of the door. The next knock was louder still.

'Gerry, I need to speak to you about the coroner's licence.'

Reluctantly, she got up off the bed, fishing for a tissue from inside the cuff of her shirt.

'Just coming,' she said.

She wiped her eyes and opened the door. She could feel his concern enfold her like a warm blanket and realised she was shivering. He took her gently by the shoulders and guided her to the bed. She felt the edge of the frame against the back of her knees and sank into the mattress. He sat down beside her, sliding his hands down her arms and taking hold of her wrists, turning her to face him. He gently caressed the mounds of her palms with his thumbs in slow circling movements. She could feel her heart begin to pound.

'I was so worried about you. Tom told me you were in a state and seemed to think it was connected to the neonate you found but I knew it couldn't be that. You must have seen loads of skeletons when you were working on the university dig at the Roman cemetery site Professor Golding used to run at Bristol. I was afraid it was about last night. I am so sorry. I didn't know how to act when we met afterwards. When I woke up this morning in bed and you were gone…' He shook his head as if to clear away the confusion. 'You see, I had too much to drink – nerves, I suppose – and was pinning my hopes on us being able to make love properly when the effects wore off. You were so sweet trying to help me and I was embarrassed that I couldn't respond to all the lovely things you did. I pretended to sleep hoping everything would be alright when we tried again.'

Relief swept over Gerry in a wave and with it came desire. She dared to look up into his eyes and was overwhelmed by the way he was looking at her. He must have seen the answer in her own eyes and leaned in to kiss her. Their lips touched, parted and their tongues met and entwined in curving arabesques of sensation. His weight shifted and they were lying side by side, hands exploring each other below the layers of clothes, finding bare skin. Impatiently, she pulled away and sat up, tugging jumper and T-shirt over her head in one swift movement. She reached behind to unclasp her bra and the straps slipped down over her shoulders. She plucked it off and threw it aside. She swung her legs over the side of the bed and stood up. Their eyes locked as she undid the button at the waistband, drew down the zip and wriggled out of her jeans and pants.

'Wait there,' he said hoarsely and she stood trembling in front of him as his gaze travelled over her body from her small white rounded breasts, tipped with ruby nipples, past the smooth curve of her stomach down to the triangle of tangled copper that lay at the top of her long-tanned thighs. She felt her cheeks grow hot at the intensity of his scrutiny. Unable to stand it any longer, she sat down again beside him on the bed.

'Now it's your turn,' she said.

She slowly undid the buttons of his shirt, peeling it back to reveal his bronze chest. She stroked the dusky nipples with her fingertips, delighted to see them contract and tighten at her touch. She bent over to taste them with her tongue and smiled as he groaned. Her fingers strayed further down, and his stomach tensed as she undid the button of his shorts and pulled down the zip. She reached inside his boxer shorts and felt he was hard and ready. Within moments, he was naked too. She gripped him lightly with her thumb and two fingers and began to move her hand up and down in a slow rhythm.

'Not yet,' he said, taking her by the waist and sitting her astride him as he lay down. She could feel his dick resting against the cleft of her buttocks. He pressed lightly on her back so she was leaning forward, her arms either side of his head supporting her weight. He took her nipples in turn into his mouth and rolled them with his tongue. She arched her back and groaned, feeling her belly contract with pleasure. His hands moved from her back to her front, over the smooth swell of her stomach, down the insides of her thighs following the line of his gaze a few minutes before. He began rubbing her gently until her breath was coming in gasps.

'Now,' she begged.

He took her by the waist again and gently raised her up, shifting her back to enter her. She bent her arms until they were skin-to-skin, mouth-to-mouth, tongues entwined. She felt him moving inside her, slowly at first, then faster. She matched his pace, stroke for stroke until they both exploded in a release of pleasure. They lay panting, exhausted, glistening with sweat. She rolled onto her side and he cradled her in his arms. Face to face, each looked deeply into the other's eyes. Any trace of embarrassment was gone.

'That was better,' he said with a grin.

'Much,' she said with an answering smile.

They lay together, side by side, in contented silence as their breathing returned to normal. The light faded in the room as the shadows lengthened outside. An owl called outside the window.

'It'll be dark soon,' he said. 'We ought to think about getting back.'

'I'm not going back to the site.'

He turned back to face her, raising himself on one elbow. 'I thought we were good now,' he said struggling to make out her expression in the gloom.

She lay on her back looking up at the ceiling. This was going to be hard, but she had to tell him if anything was going to come of their feelings for each other. He waited patiently.

'You weren't the reason I needed to leave,' she said at last, struggling to sit up. 'Look, this would be easier if we were dressed.'

'I don't agree,' he said, pulling her back down beside him. 'After we've been so close physically, the last thing we need is to be separated if you need to say something difficult. Tell me what bothered you so much that you wanted to leave the dig.'

'It wasn't the dig I was leaving. I just couldn't stay on the site.'

'Why ever not? Did Tom say or do something to upset you?'

'Of course not. He's a lovely guy. No, it was what I found today in the foundation trench.'

He frowned, wondering what on earth she was talking about then light dawned. 'Surely you weren't spooked by the presence of a skeleton? I thought you'd dug up loads of skeletons. Professor Golding used a Roman cemetery as your university's training dig.'

'Not any skeleton, that skeleton, or rather, the fact it was a baby's skeleton.'

'I don't see the difference...' he began to say.

'It's personal,' she interrupted. She could see that he still had no idea what she was talking about. She would have to come right out and say it. 'I lost a baby. Two years ago. Just before finals.' She buried her face against him and felt the wetness of her tears on his chest.

'Oh my god. I am so sorry to be such an insensitive idiot.' He tightened his arms around her and began to rock her, to and fro. Her body shook with sobs as she howled and let out all the misery she had been feeling for the last two years. When the storm had subsided, he left her curled up on the bed and went to the bathroom. He came back with a damp flannel and tenderly wiped her reddened eyes and tear-stained face.

She smiled sweetly at him, grateful for his concern. 'I feel silly to be making such a fuss about an old skeleton.'

'No, I can see it must have been an awful shock and clearly, triggered all your memories of what must have been a traumatic experience. Did Professor Golding know?'

'No one did.'

'Not even the father?'

'Richard? He was long gone. He left as soon as I told him I was pregnant.'

'What a bastard!'

'That pretty well sums him up, though I was better off without him. He had been messing me about for most of the two years we were together. He couldn't keep away from other women. He always said he was sorry, but it didn't stop him doing it again. Like a fool, I forgave him every time. It was only when he had finally gone that I realised what an idiot I had been. I was really happy at the thought of having a child, even OK with being a single mum, and as the birth wasn't due until well after finals, I thought I would be able to get stuck into the first couple of months of my PhD – I had funding and everything.' She could feel the tears coming again.

'So, what happened to the PhD?' he asked.

'I lost the funding because of my poor results. You see, I began to miscarry the day before my finals. When I arrived for the first exam, I was in a complete state and could barely write my name let alone answer the questions on the paper. Professor Golding told me privately afterwards that the moderators had only given me a pass because my dissertation was so good. The funding was withdrawn because I didn't even make an upper second, let alone the first-class degree I was hoping for.'

Peter now had the answer to what had been puzzling him ever since Gerry's CV had arrived on his desk. She had such an excellent reference from the Professor, he had no qualms about taking her on but had wondered why someone who was considered so bright had got only an average degree. At least, she seemed to be calmer now. What a terrible thing to have to face alone. It must have been a relief to talk about it after so long. He was glad he was the first person she told. Her distress had brought on a desire to protect her that was rapidly developing into a desire to make love to her. When did crying become so sexy? His feelings for her seemed to be deepening by the minute. Better get out before they overwhelmed him. The last thing she needed right now was more sex and he didn't think he could hold out if he stayed. He took her hands in his again.

'Look, I'd better leave before they throw me out. Single rooms are supposed to be single occupancy. Will you promise to come back tomorrow? I've managed to get an osteo-archae-ologist to come in the morning to lift the bones and take them away to the lab. I've worked with her before. She's very good at her job and should have finished and be gone by twelve.'

He was already putting on his boxers and shorts. Gerry felt a pang of disappointment. She wanted to make love to him again. She could feel herself getting wet at the thought. Although she was emotionally drained, it was as if a great weight had been lifted from her heart and the relief was acting like an aphrodisiac. Still, she must look a fright after all that crying. Her eyes were still stinging with tears and no man she had ever known had found a weeping woman sexy.

'Yes, you'd better go. I'll come back to the site after lunch.'

He picked up his shirt off the floor and bent to kiss her. She was tempted to pull him down on top of her and start again but managed to resist. The door clicked shut and she was alone.

Chapter 14

*Suetonius had assembled a force of 10,000 men including
the fourteenth legion, part of the twentieth and auxiliaries
from the nearest forts in a narrow ravine with a wood at one
end. In front was a plain where the rebels were camped. The
position was perfect for a pitched battle with no cover for
the enemy and no risk of ambush. He arranged the army
carefully. The legionaries were in in the middle with auxiliaries either side and the cavalry on the wings. The British
army in contrast were milling about in a state of disorder.
There were so many of them and they were so sure of victory
that they had brought their women in wagons, which had
been drawn up around the edges of the plain so their wives
could see their success in battle.*

Tacitus. Annals 34.1-8

It was a good place to fight, thought Marcus. Suetonius Paulinus had chosen to meet Boudicca in a narrow ravine. At one
end was a thick wood. The rebel tribes swarmed over the plain
at the other end in a confused jumble of chariots, horsemen
and warriors on foot. Their numerical superiority would be
wasted as the fighting front was constrained. The general had
arranged his men with precision. The legions were drawn up
in the centre with the auxiliaries on the flanks and the cavalry
in front. Before engaging, he had called Marcus to his side to
explain his strategy.

'We have met their tactics before and understand now how
to defeat them. They will try to rout us with the chariots, but
we will stand firm and the front ranks will release their spears
to bring down the horses. They will run into each other in the
cramped conditions and lose courage and retreat, but they will

be cut off by their own warriors running up behind them and in the confusion, we will cut them down with our swords.'

Marcus nodded to show he understood. His throat was too dry to speak.

'Don't worry, boy. You'll be fine,' said Paulinus.

***

Boudicca drove her chariot up and down the line; her eyes wild with anticipation. She drew up in front of the assembled army. Her auburn hair cascaded over her brightly striped tunic, and the golden torc at her throat glittered in the autumn sunshine. Her voice was harsh and carried through the still air.

'This is not the first time I have led you into battle. You look at me and see a woman, but I have the heart of a warrior. My ancestors were mighty but I am mightier still. Like you, I am fighting for freedom – and vengeance. The Romans have robbed us of the right to rule ourselves. They make free with our women, raped my daughters and flogged me like a slave. You know what it is to be slaves, deceived by false promises. We have been despised and trampled underfoot. The Romans have embezzled our wealth, taxed us beyond endurance and made us work in their fields and factories. Death would be better, although, even in death, we are not free whilst these vermin pollute our earth. Now the time has come to shake off this yoke. You have no reason to fear the Romans. We are greater in number, stronger and braver. They are weak and need to protect themselves with helmets, body armour and walls while we need only our tents and shields. They cannot survive without shade and covering, kneaded bread and wine and oil. We know this land but to them it is alien and hostile. They are hares and foxes. We are dogs and wolves.'

A hare appeared suddenly from beneath the wheels of her chariot and ran off to the left. Boudicca was ecstatic. What a stroke of luck! She raised her hand towards the heavens and cried, 'See how Andraste foretells our victory!'

The tribesmen roared and brandished their spears. She wheeled her chariot around, and they poured behind her as she charged into the mouth of the ravine.

Paulinus waited until they were in range. At his order, the standard-bearer raised the Eagle. This was the signal. Spears rained down terrifying the approaching horses, and the drivers in the enemy chariots brought their horses to a halt and tried to back into the men behind as predicted. The cavalry charged in wedge formation, scattering the native troops with the force of their advance. The legionaries fell in behind them. Slowly, but inexorably, the British were driven back. The retreat turned into a rout, but the end of the ravine was blocked by the wagons of the camp followers who had followed the tribesman to better see their victory.

The Roman soldiers had no thought of mercy. They had heard rumours of seventy thousand massacred in Camulodunum, Verulamium and Londinium, of men women and children put to death by fire and sword. When Paulinus gave the order to disengage, the ground was slippery with the blood of the thousands of rebels who lay dead.

But Boudicca was not among them. Through sheer recklessness, she had reached the end of the wood behind the Roman lines at the end of the first charge but was now isolated. Her chariot had shattered against a rocky outcrop and the horses had escaped. She realised her part in the battle was over. Valda and Mardunad were slumped together at her feet – dead or unconscious, she didn't care. They were no use to her now. The Roman soldiers, after pressing forward against her people, were now some distance away. She was just yards from the nearest oak. She dropped to the ground and ran half-crouching to the safety of its canopy, leaving her daughters to fend for themselves.

Valda, battered and bruised by the buffeting she had received as the wheels bumped over the rough ground, staggered to her feet and watched her mother disappear into the shadow of the trees. She looked down at her sister. Mardunad's head was twisted unnaturally to one side. Valda hesitated but only for a moment. She wanted to cradle that broken body in her arms and wail in despair, but her sister was beyond her help and she had no time to waste. She winced as she stepped down onto the soggy ground. The pain was so great, she wondered if her leg was broken. She tested it again with her weight. The pain eased to a bearable ache, and she moved away from the safety of the chariot. The fighting had moved onto the distant plain, and there was no one to see her as she limped after her mother.

Boudicca was some way ahead, but Valda did not need the trampled bracken and broken branches to see which way she had gone. The queen was talking to herself. Snatches of what she was saying drifted back on the breeze.

'He wants blood, must give him blood. So thirsty. I must drink. He must drink.'

The same words muttered over and over again. She was crazed with her desire for vengeance. She must be stopped.

Valda caught up with her in a clearing. Boudicca had sat down on a fallen tree and was twisting her hands together as she recited the strange litany.

'Who wants blood, mother?'

Boudicca swung around in alarm, but relaxed when she recognised her daughter.

'Camulus, of course,' she replied as if to a small child. 'Our god of war needs more blood. I am thirsty too. We must drink.'

Valda was shocked at the way her mother looked now. The orgy of destruction had finally taken its toll. Her mouth was slack and a thin stream of spittle ran from the corner of her mouth to her chin. The whites of her eyes were laced with red and the pupils huge and dark. Boudicca grabbed her daughter's arm and plucked at her wrist as if she was trying to tug out the veins that pulsed below the white skin.

Valda attempted to pull her arm away but Boudicca was too strong. The girl reached out for a branch to steady herself, and her hand closed on a spray of purple berries. She felt the juice running into her clenched fist as her mother dragged her nearer. She looked back to see what bush the berries had come from. When she realised what she was holding, she squeezed harder and allowed her mother to pull her closer.

'I will give you blood,' said Valda softly.

Boudicca bared her teeth in readiness, but as she bent forward to bite the proffered wrist, Valda thrust her other hand into her mother's open mouth. Boudicca swallowed involuntarily as the juice tricked into the back of her throat. She looked at Valda in surprise.

'Not blood,' was all she had time to say before she screamed and doubled up clutching her stomach. She rocked back and forth on the tree trunk, toppled over and lay rigid, drumming her feet against the ground. Valda wondered if it would ever end but within minutes it was over. She sat down on the tree trunk and looked at the still figure. She felt empty of all feeling and very cold. She began to shiver.

***

Marcus had been ordered to check the woods for any survivors. He was pretty sure that Paulinus wasn't expecting him to find any but had wanted him out the way for a while for reasons of his own. He was glad of a chance to think. He stopped in shock at the edge of a clearing. He recognised the body immediately. He rushed over to the still form then saw the girl sitting nearby. Her face was white and pinched and her eyes were blank. It took a moment for him to realise who she was. Then he remembered the slave's lewd jokes about the youngest one being so skinny and all the horror of that night came flooding back. She was one of Boudicca's daughters, but what was her name? Valda, that was her name. He felt a rush of compassion for the way her body was shaking and went down on one knee beside her.

'Don't be afraid. I won't hurt you. Your name is Valda, isn't it?' Then he saw that she had recognised him too.

'You raped my cousin.' Her voice was flat and devoid of emotion.

'No, you've got it wrong. I was trying to help her.'

'Will you rape me too?' He was shocked at the conversational tone.

'No, I told you, I was trying to help her.' She seemed uninterested and looked over at her mother. 'I had to kill her. She was mad. I wanted to stop the madness so no one else was hurt.'

Marcus, for the first time in his life, had no idea what to do. If he took her to Paulinus, she would either be killed outright or sent as a hostage to Rome. She had suffered enough. He remembered with shame hearing her cries that dreadful night and doing nothing to help her or her sister. Then he had an idea.

'I know where you can find Gwenneth,' he said. 'If you go now, whilst the legions are preparing camp, no one will see you or follow you.'

'Why would you help me?'

He didn't know how to explain something he could barely understand himself. If he said she felt like kin to him now, she would think him mad. He had to get her to believe he wanted her to go to Gwenneth to take a message and in a sense that was true. Sparing her cousin would show something about the depth of his feeling for Gwenneth and the fact that he had sent a member of her family to say he would soon be back might help to convince her it was true. He started to explain where Gwenneth was hiding but Valda interrupted.

'What about my mother? I killed her. There is no place now for me with my people.'

'No one will ever know. I will tell my commander I found her here alone. They will think she has poisoned herself.'

For the first time, Marcus saw her smile and realised she was very pretty and very like her cousin.

'No one who knows my mother will believe that.'

'It is a very Roman thing to do,' agreed Marcus – so the army will believe it. It is also highly likely that your people will not, but they are sure to blame it on us – why would they ever believe it of you?'

She looked at him doubtfully, but he could tell she realised there wasn't really any other choice. When he was sure she

117

understood where Gwenneth was to be found, he helped her to stand up.

'Now go.'

She nodded and limped off through the wood. Marcus watched until she was out of sight. He felt overwhelmed with relief. Now he could go back to Paulinus and carry out his duties without having to worry about Gwenneth. The rebellion was over, and it wouldn't be long before he was allowed some leave and could go back to her again.

Chapter 15

The soil is fertile and can be cultivated but it is not suitable for the olive, the vine, and other fruits which prefer a warmer climate. The crops need to be sown early and so not ripen until later in the year.

Tacitus Agricola 12

Gwenneth waited for Marcus to come back to her. Every morning, she walked along by the river until she came to the place where it met the road to Camulodunum. There, she would stay for several hours looking for the cloud of dust that would signal his return. Every evening, she would cry on the heap of bracken that served as a bed in the makeshift shelter until she fell asleep. As the days passed, she would leave it later and later to go to the road to look for the man who never came.

At first, she was angry, imagining that he was spending his time drinking with his friends. Then she worried he had been attacked by thieves or been thrown from his horse. Eventually, she gave up hope altogether and stopped going to wait for him.

Nearly six weeks had passed since the day Marcus had left before she realised she was going to have a child. Her immediate reaction was to go in search of herbs that might kill it, but she didn't really know how much and what to take and was afraid of giving birth to a monster. She thought of killing herself, but as she stood on the edge of a high escarpment, her nerve failed her. Then, at the height of her despair, she suddenly remembered how kind Bodwyn had been. Surely, he would help her? His farm was quite remote, and he may not have heard of her banishment, and even if he had, when he saw her condition, he might take pity on her.

She collected her things together and bundled them up into a blanket with enough food and water for the journey. Before leaving, she pulled the shelter apart and stamped on the wattle hurdles until all that was left was a heap of wood fit only for kindling. Once she was satisfied that not a trace remained, she left without a backward glance, glad that the long period of waiting was over.

***

The farmstead seemed to be deserted. Gwenneth hid in the ditch by the gate and watched the hut. She had seen no sign of anyone since she arrived a couple of hours earlier. No smoke was rising through the thatched roof although it was nearly sunset. She crept from her hiding place and drew closer. She called out but no one answered. Not even a dog barked. She stood up and went up to the door and drew aside the skins that sealed the entrance. Inside it was dark, but once her eyes got used to the gloom, it was clear that no one had lived there for a while. There were no signs of struggle and the contents looked orderly enough. The fire was made up ready to light and a cauldron was suspended on the tripod that straddled the hearth. The skins were tidily arranged in the curtained off sleeping area.

Gwenneth sat down on one of the beds and tried to decide what to do. She heard the cattle lowing outside and wondered when they had last been milked. If was more than a few days, they would be dry. The pigs and sheep would have been able to forage, but soon, the crops would need to be harvested. Suddenly, the solution seemed obvious. She could stay here and do what was necessary to keep the farm running until Bodwyn returned. He would be so grateful to her; he would be bound to let her stay on at least until after the baby was born. Tomorrow, she would put her plan into action, but now, she was hungry. She lit the fire and soon, a potful of gruel was bubbling away over the flames.

***

Gwenneth spent the following day looking around to assess what needed to be done. She saw that the weeds had grown high and the ripening wheat was being choked by fat hen and bindweed. Poppies and corn cockles grew in abundance, splashes of scarlet and blue against the gold. It was too late to hoe without disturbing the spreading roots of the crop. She would have to pick the ears by hand so there were not too many weeds in the harvest and the poisonous plants were excluded. Just as well, as she was not used to using a billhook. Luckily, there was no trace of charlock, so the fields had been tended until at least early summer. It would be impossible for her to reap all the corn under cultivation. Bodwyn was growing much more than he and his wife would need. He must be trading the surplus with the army. She would only be able to harvest enough for herself and their needs with sufficient to plant for next year's crop. She would have to start as soon as the first spikes were ready.

As she had feared, the milking cows were dry. Their calves had stopped suckling, so it had not taken long. There was nothing she could do until the following spring except to keep the beasts alive over the winter. There was enough rough grazing for many of them, and if the weaker ones should die, then it would help the survival of the rest of the herd. Only a few sheep grazed on the valley slopes. The ewes were all dry too, but as she had hoped, they had been sheared before the farmstead was abandoned. Some were limping because their hooves were overgrown, but it didn't take long to trim off the excess. She had done it many times before, and she flipped the animals onto their backs with ease. Whilst they were lying immobile in this position, she checked for signs of injury and illness before paring down their hooves with the knife that always hung at her waist.

By the time she had finished, it was getting late. She returned to the hut and lit the fire to warm the gruel from the night before. Her appetite had gone, and she had to fight against a feeling of nausea as she ate. She knew women in her

121

condition often felt sick at first, but she had not realised it would affect the taste of everything she ate. If this continued, she worried about the baby growing inside her. Would it starve? What about her own health? If she got too weak, how would she manage to keep the farm going? That night, she lay awake for many hours tangling herself up in the furs as she moved around trying to get to sleep.

***

In the morning, her natural optimism resurfaced. Despite the taste of bile in her mouth she managed to finish off the rest of the gruel. She dressed in her outer clothes and pulled on her leather boots and went outside. It was going to be a fine autumn day when the mist rising over the river had been burnt off by the rising sun. She went down to the stream to wash her face and empty her bladder. Her skin tingled at the touch of the freezing water. It felt good to be alive. She went back to find the tools she would need to prepare for the harvest.

A wattle fence enclosed the house and yard and built into it were the sheds which housed the farm equipment. Inside one, she found a pick and a shovel. She carried them over to a patch of scrubland and began to dig. All day, she worked in the hot sun until her back was aching and her hands were stiff and sore. By the time dusk fell, she had opened up a shallow pit in the chalk bedrock. The sides curved in from a wide flat base to the narrower opening. The upcast lay in a neat pile, which she was going to use to cover the corn and then seal it with a layer of clay to prevent water and air getting in to spoil it.

The moon hung huge and red on the horizon as she made her way back to the house. Her appetite had returned as the day wore on, but she hardly had the strength to eat some strong cheese washed down by a mug of beer before collapsing exhausted on the bed. Unlike the night before, she fell at once into a deep and dreamless sleep.

Over the next few days, the good weather held, and she picked the corn from sunrise to sunset, her mind in a trance, induced by the monotony of hand-to-corn-to-basket as she trudged from field to field. She saw nothing but the next ear to be plucked. From time to time, she went in amongst the cattle and took blood from one of them to drink. She had found it was the only form of food she could eat which did not make her retch and which gave he enough energy to keep on with the backbreaking work.

After she had filled the pit with corn, she used the sacks she had found in the sheds to store the corn. When she judged there was enough to feed her, and maybe Bodwyn and his wife, through the winter, she started cutting the stalks for bedding and animal fodder and put them into one of the out houses. For twenty days, she worked, stopping only to eat and sleep.

***

Gwenneth woke up one morning to hear the water dripping from the eaves. The onset of rain meant she could get the rest her body craved at last. She fell asleep again and did not wake up until the following day.

It was hunger that woke her. The nausea had finally disappeared and eating was a pleasure again. She raided Bodwyn's stores for good things to eat and settled down to a huge breakfast of smoked meat, dried fruit, cheese, oatcakes and honey. With her stomach full, she felt ready for anything. It was time to explore the countryside and try to find out what was happening in the wider world. The rain had stopped, so she packed a leather bag with provisions and tramped off through the mud, heading north towards the borders of the Iceni kingdom.

The grey clouds rolled back and the sun shone down from a solitary patch of blue sky. Gwenneth had reached the edge of a low escarpment. Across the valley, she could see the fort of Durobrivae. She wondered why there was none of the usual activity outside the earthen ramparts, and she could not see the Eagle rising above the timber palisade. Beyond the fort, a river meandered through the woods. The leaves of the trees had turned to the browns and golds of autumn. In the distance, she could see smoke drifting in a blue haze. She realised she was close to her first refuge after her banishment. Had he come back after all? All her bitterness and anger vanished as she scrambled down the slope, desperate to see her young Roman again.

Chapter 16

Although he was a brilliant administrator his treatment of
the defeated Britons was excessively harsh as if they had
done him a personal injury. Consequently he was replaced
by Petronius Turpilianus who was more merciful and as he
had not been witness to the atrocities was more inclined to
forgive our enemies. He brought back order to the province
without undertaking any further military expeditions and
then handed over to Trebellius Maximus.

Tacitus. Agricola XVI

'Marcus!' Gwenneth cried as she burst out of the woods and
ran towards the hooded figure bent over the fire. Then she
stopped dead. The face that turned towards her was not that of
her lover, but she knew it all the same, although the dimples
she remembered had been replaced with deep lines that etched
a path from nose to chin on each side of her mouth. The vel-
vety brown eyes that had sparkled with laughter were dull and
bloodshot.

'Valda?' she whispered, shocked by the emaciated crea-
ture that her cousin had become. She knelt down on the grass
and took the girl gently into her arms, horrified to feel the outline of bones even through the thickness of the woollen cloak.
Valda started to shake and then the tears came. Tenderly,
Gwenneth rocked her back and forth like a baby, crooning
words of comfort, aware of an intense feeling of disappointment mixed with confusion at finding her cousin here instead
of Marcus.

At last, the sobbing stopped. Gwenneth rummaged in her
bag and handed Valda some of the dried meat she had brought
with her. The girl tore at it with her teeth like a ravenous dog

in between gulps from the water bottle Gwenneth proffered. Then she settled back against the tree and closed her eyes.

'I killed my mother.'

This was so far from any explanation that made sense that Gwenneth said nothing, although her mind was racing.

'I came to find you,' said Valda. 'He said you would be here, but he was wrong. I have been waiting and waiting but you didn't come.' She spoke like a lost child.

Gwenneth took her hand and stroked it as her cousin began to cry again.

'Who said I would be here?' she asked gently.

'The man who hurt you.'

Gwenneth raised her hand involuntarily to the scar on her temple left by the burn. How could the druid have known she would be here? Of course – he could read the runes. Her heart began to thud. The searchers would be out. She got to her feet and looked around in panic. They might even now be in the woods. She must leave immediately. But what about Valda? The girl seemed to have lost her wits. She couldn't abandon her in the woods. It looked as if she hadn't eaten for weeks and her shoes were torn and bloodstained. What did she mean when she said she had killed her mother? Was Boudicca really dead? By her own daughter's hand? If it were true, why was Valda still alive? These questions teemed through her mind, but she realised that she would not get any answers from Valda in her present state. All that mattered now was to get out of this place as quickly as possible. She sat down again next to her cousin and put her arm around her shoulders.

'Would you like to come home with me?'

'Where do you live?'

'Not too far away. Do you think you can walk if I help you?'

'I'll try,' said Valda like a little girl trying to please her mother.

Gwenneth pulled her up and with their arms about each other's waists, they set off along the riverbank.

***

The sun had set long before they reached the scarp and the moon was overhead when Gwenneth at last saw the conical roof of the farm silhouetted against the deep blue of the night sky. Valda had begged to be allowed to rest after nearly every mile, although she had leaned on Gwenneth all the way. Both of them were exhausted. They crossed the causeway that led over the ditch into the porch and collapsed just inside the threshold.

Gwenneth awoke bathed in sunlight. The warm rays poured in thorough the open door, illuminating the dust that hung in the still air. She wondered what she was doing on the ground then she saw Valda beside her and remembered everything. She stood up slowly, stiff and sore from lying on the earthen floor all night. He stomach was cramped with hunger, and she set about preparing breakfast for them both.

Over the next few days, good food, sleep and the gentle encouragement of her cousin did much to restore Valda to normality, but she never forgot the fear she had seen in Gwenneth's eyes when she had said who had sent her into the woods. That Roman soldier must have been lying. He had raped her cousin. She resolved then not to speak of him again. That meant she would also have to say nothing about the battle and her mother's death. It would be too complicated to explain.

Gwenneth was relieved to find her cousin's sanity returning and was afraid to probe any deeper into the mystery of Boudicca's death in case it brought back the madness. Constrained from speaking about what mattered most and recognising in each other a deep grief which made light-hearted chatter impossible, the two young women mostly passed the time in silence but found a way to offer companionship without words in carrying out their daily tasks around the farmstead until it was time to kill the first of the animals.

Gwenneth had strung up one of the pigs and Valda came out of the hut just as her cousin drew her knife across its throat. As the blood streamed into the bucket, Valda started to scream. She grabbed the knife from Gwenneth and held it against her wrist. She called on Camulos and promised him blood. Gwenneth caught her hand as she began sawing frantically through the woollen cloth of her tunic and managed to stop her before she broke the skin. After that, she made sure Valda was out of sight before slaughtering any more of their stock.

***

Autumn passed into winter. Bad weather drove the girls indoors. They kept the fire burning all day, and the smoke that wafted up through the hole in the roof cured the joints of meat that hung above the hearth. At first, Gwenneth passed the time working the tall loom to weave brightly coloured cloaks, tunics and blankets, but as the snow deepened, her increasing bulk made it uncomfortable to stand for long periods and her fingers were sometimes so swollen, she was unable to work the threads with her usual deft movements. She spent hours sitting by the fire, staring into the flames and dreaming about the lovely summer days she had spent with Marcus. She would look up to find Valda watching her, then self-conscious of her swelling waist, she would take up a skin from one of the slaughtered animals and pretend to work it to hide the evidence. Nothing had been said between them about the coming baby. Gwenneth did not know how to explain she was carrying the baby of a Roman soldier, and Valda thought her cousin did not want to be reminded of her rape.

***

Gradually, the days grew longer. One morning, Gwenneth went outside and found the snow was flecked with green where the grass had pushed through. She felt restless and decided to go in search of firewood to replenish their dwindling log pile. Valda tried to dissuade her as she guessed she was near her time, but Gwenneth dismissed her worries as needless fussing and left with a width of cloth slung across her shoulder to carry back whatever she found. Valda watched her trudge through the snow until she disappeared over the horizon then went inside to make things ready for the birth.

Drawn by an impulse she refused to acknowledge, Gwenneth headed south towards the fort. Again, she stood on the edge of the scarp and looked across the valley. Now, the fort was bustling with activity. The ramparts were being extended to increase the enclosed area and the soldiers were raising the height of the timber palisade. The section nearest to her had been completed, so the interior was hidden from view. She wondered why the fort was being made bigger and was considering going further along the ridge to where she would be able to catch a glimpse of what was going on inside. Then she thought better of it. They needed the firewood not news about the Roman army. She climbed carefully down the slope and waddled to the edge of the wood. When her sling was full, she stretched to relieve the aching muscles in her back and looked up at the skyline.

A rider was up on the ridge. She drew her hood over her head and hurried as best as she could deep into the shadow of the trees. She turned to look again, narrowing her eyes against the glare of the sun. The rider had gone. She felt a sharp pain in her belly. It was time to go home.

Chapter 17

Petilius Cerealis was made governor.
Tacitus. Agricola VIII

Marcus rode back to the fort. He was getting tired of searching. Today, he had thought he had finally found her. He had glimpsed a flash of gold amongst the trees and his pulse had quickened. Then he had seen it was just a fat old woman waddling around collecting firewood, enveloped in a dull grey woollen cloak with a hood that she pulled back over her head as he watched. The hair colour was similar, but Gwenneth had been light on her feet and graceful as a young fawn. She would never waddle! Remembering her body made him long to feel her in his arms again and kiss her sweet mouth.

He reached the gates of the fort and stopped to watch the soldiers at work on the new buildings. He had been lucky to get a posting here. He should have left the province with Paulinus when the governor was recalled to Rome in disgrace, but had been granted leave to stay, at least until Paulinus' replacement arrived, and maybe longer if the new man liked him. They had needed someone in Durobrivae to organise the supply of construction materials with all the re-building required, and he had jumped at the chance to be so close to the place where he and Gwenneth had fallen in love.

He watched the men working, but his thoughts were far away, locked in that day when he had first gone to look for her after taking up his new post. He had ridden out from the fort, down into the valley and along the riverbank. He could still recall his stomach churning in anticipation of seeing her again. He replayed the scene in his mind: how he had dismounted when he was still a little way from the clearing and tethered his horse before creeping along the edge of the wood, his heart pounding; the disbelief when he couldn't see the little makeshift shelter and the feeling he must have made a mistake and come to the wrong place. He had searched up and down both sides of the stream, frantically looking for a sign that it had been real.

He remembered how he had sat for a long time on the grass with his head in his hands. All through the misery of his ride to Deva, his fear and anger on the battlefield and his horror at the devastation wrought by Boudicca on the towns of Camulodunum, Verulamium and Londinium, the hope of seeing her again had kept him going. It had helped him to cope as he watched his own comrades ravage the countryside in retaliation, on the orders of their commander. It had been his consolation as day-by-day, he lost his respect for Paulinus, who was behaving like a barbarian instead of the wise Roman leader he had hero-worshipped since he was a young boy. He had been glad when the emperor had sent orders for the governor to return on the pretext of him being responsible for a disastrous loss of ships. Paulinus had blamed his disgrace on the plotting of the new procurator, Classicianus, who had the ear of the emperor, Nero. Whatever the reason, Marcus had been glad to see the back of him. There would have been no hope of peace if Paulinus had stayed in office after the way he treated the native Britons.

A shout dragged Marcus back to the present. He was blocking the way of a cart full of timber. He pulled his horse aside and followed the cart into the fort. He rode to the room in the barrack block he shared with two of the Spanish cavalry stationed at Durobrivae and made his horse comfortable in the partitioned off area they used as a stable. It was a temporary arrangement, and he found it was quite a lonely life as his roommates resented him being billeted with them since he was not one of their regiment. There was nowhere else he could stay, as he needed his horse with him in case he had to leave at a moment's notice to sort out a delivery. He envied the other administrative staff who were office-based and slept in the headquarters building.

He went to the mess to grab something to eat. That they were still on full rations was a tribute to the organisational skills of the quartermaster here at Durobrivae. Famine was widespread. The native Britons had neglected the harvest, confident they would be able to loot what they needed from the army granaries when the Romans had been driven out of the province. Now they were starving. Since Marcus had discovered Gwenneth was missing, he was desperately worried. He had thought she would be safe in the woods, as she had shown herself to be an accomplished hunter and skilled at gathering hedgerow fruits and nuts. Although they had not known each other long, he admired her resourcefulness and had no doubt she would have the sense to smoke meat and store enough food to keep for herself and him when he returned. Now he pictured her, roaming alone and friendless with nothing to eat. He never once thought she was dead. That was why he still, after all these months, rode out whenever he could to try and find her. He thought he had visited every homestead within a day's ride and was beginning to think she must have gone back north to Boudicca's former stronghold despite her fear of the druidic curse. But there was one place he had missed: a small hut at the end of an overgrown track, hidden from the road by a dense thicket and less than two hours away from where he sat eating that evening in early spring.

***

The pains were coming with a frequency and severity that made Gwenneth gasp. She did not know how she found the strength to reach Bodwyn's farm. Climbing up the slope to the edge of the scarp had been agonising. She had stopped to rest as soon as she felt a contraction starting, terrified of slipping. Once she reached the top, she had tried to escape the pain by cutting off her conscious thoughts and drifting through a dream world in her mind.

Valda heard her groans and came running out to meet her. Gwyneth flinched as her cousin put out her arm to help her over the threshold. She remembered how Valda had reacted to the sight of blood. Every woman bled during childbirth. She would be helpless if Valda lost her mind again. She looked into the young woman's eyes and her fear dissipated. They were clear and calm with no trace of madness.

'Don't be afraid, my darling. I know what to do. See, everything is ready.'

Gwyneth allowed herself to be led to a bed of sheepskins piled up near the hearth. She sank down into the soft wool and sipped gratefully at the warm aromatic drink she was handed. The pain eased. She could still feel it but it seemed to be coming from a distance. She wondered how Valda knew what to do. Valda seemed to guess her thoughts.

'The drink is made of the herbs they gave me after I was raped, but milder, so you can still feel to push,' she said as she pressed lightly on Gwenneth's swollen belly. She felt the taut muscles relaxing as the drink took effect. She was satisfied she had made the drink just the right strength. A little pain was necessary – it would help her cousin know what to do – but too much would make her tense and hold up the birth.

'I need to push,' said Gwenneth. She raised herself into a squatting position. Beads of sweat stood out against her pale skin. A few moments later, her belly heaved and she gritted her teeth and pushed hard as she felt her insides contracting. She pushed again, grunting with the effort…again…and again…and again.

'I think it's coming,' she said at last with a groan and started panting. Valda checked between her legs. She could see a mass of black hair soaked with blood and mucus.

'Once more, darling, and make this your strongest yet,' she coaxed.

Gwenneth took a deep breath, pressed her chin down into her chest and did as she was told. She screamed as she felt herself tearing, then fell back. Valda eased the tiny scrap as it twisted its way out into the world and laid it on its mother's body.

Gwenneth looked down in wonder. When it was growing inside her, she had always imagined the baby as part of herself.

Even when she felt the butterfly caress of its tiny limbs, her imagination had failed to associate the movements with a separate entity. Yet, from the moment of his birth, he was entirely himself. Not her but part of her and part of Marcus too. She raised him to her breast and he suckled greedily. His wizened face, the forehead wrinkled in a frown, was old and young, ugly and beautiful. His thick dark hair hid the pulse where the skull was not yet sealed but she could feel it throbbing when she stroked his head. His eyes were closed in ecstasy and Gwenneth felt an answering thrill as his pursed lips tugged at her nipple for the first milk. After a few minutes, he fell asleep and Gwenneth curled her body protectively around him and did the same.

Valda looked on whilst mother and baby slept. The mist that had clouded her mind had gone, and she could think clearly again. She thought about the battle and the terrible days that followed. She traced the thin scars on her wrist with her thumbs. No wonder she had lost her mind. It was too hard for her to accept just what she had done. How had she survived the horror and come to this place? Then she remembered the young man. The young man who had a finger missing. He had told her to come here. He had given her a message. He had said she must tell her cousin he loved her. But that didn't make any sense. He had hurt her cousin. He had raped her. Now she had given birth to a bastard, not only a bastard but a half-Roman bastard. Poor little thing. He would always be an outcast.

Just then, the baby whimpered and Gwenneth stirred in her sleep. Valda hastily went over to pick up the child so his mother would not wake. He snuggled in against her shoulder and she felt a wave of tenderness flood through her body. She was overwhelmed with a fierce desire to protect the little boy. She made up her mind that he would never lack for anything it was in her power to provide.

***

The next few days were hard. The ewes had started to lamb, the cows to calf and the fields had to be ploughed ready for the seed corn to be sown. The young women worked from dawn to dusk and sometimes through the night. Valda tended to the animals as Gwenneth would have to break off what she was doing whenever the baby wanted to feed so it made more sense to work in the fields, although, it was physically more exhausting. She strapped the baby to her back and used both hands to steer the heavy wooden ard and keep it pressed down in the earth. She prepared only enough ground to sow the corn which she and Valda would need for the coming year and fill the pit again with seed.

One morning when Gwenneth put the baby to her breast, he screamed and tugged and could not settle.

'Why is he crying?' she asked Valda, starting to cry herself.

'I think you may have lost your milk,' said Valda quietly. 'I was afraid this might happen. You have been working so hard.'

'What can I do? He is too young to live without milk,' Gwenneth said in despair. She looked down at her breasts which were no longer swollen. Her nipples were dry, although, usually the baby's cries were enough to draw drops of milk onto the surface.

Without a word, Valda dipped a beaker into the water that was boiling in the cauldron ready for their morning drink then disappeared outside. When she came back, the beaker was brimming with milk, still warm from the ewe.

'He can't swallow from a cup,' said Gwenneth in a panic.

'I know,' said Valda. She took a scrap of thin leather from the work basket by the hearth, where it had been left from the previous evening, and pierced it with a needle then wrapped it round the beaker and secured it with a few stitches leaving a small bulge in the top. She went over to where Gwenneth was sitting and took the baby in the crook of her arm, turned the beaker upside down and shook it. Milk dribbled from the hole in the leather into the baby's mouth. The howling stopped as if by magic.

'How did you know what to do?' asked Gwenneth in amazement.

'I have seen it done before with a lamb that had lost its mother. I wasn't sure if it would work, but he seems happy enough.'

It was true. The baby was sucking contentedly on the substitute teat. Soon, the milk was all gone and the baby asleep in Valda's lap.

After that episode, Valda started to do more and more for the baby. Gwenneth was pleased to let her. In other circumstances, her closest kinswoman would have become a wet nurse and foster mother, but in those circumstances, the baby would also have had a father. This baby would never know his father. His father would also never know that this baby had been born. When she allowed herself to think of him, her sadness would become unbearable and all she wanted to do was lie down and weep. She had thought he loved her as much as she had loved him, and yet, he had abandoned her. She couldn't think of a single thing that would have kept him from coming back. Unless he was dead. Maybe the druid had found him and completed the rite.

Valda saw her cousin's unhappiness and her anger for the Roman soldier grew with each passing day. If she ever found him, she would kill him. He had ruined Gwenneth's life and one day, he would pay.

Chapter 18

*Once the governor had left on campaign the Britons were
free to discuss their grievances and as they compared the
wrongs inflicted on them they became angry with both the
civil and military rulers, one for taking their wealth and the
other for taking their children to serve in the army which
had more Britons in it than native Romans. They said to
each other that they could not even feel respect for their con-
querors as the better men as they were effeminate cowards.*
                                            Tacitus Agricola XV

'It's time that child had a name,' said Valda as she watched
Gwenneth playing a game with the baby. He smiled as he pad-
dled on her lap whilst she held him underneath his arms and
blew on his tummy. His mother held him up in the air and
shook him gently continuing the game as if she had not heard
her cousin.

'It is time he was named,' Valda said again.

Gwenneth sat her baby back on her knee and looked up at
last. There was a determined light in her green eyes.

'It is custom for the father to name the child.'

Valda sprang to her feet, her eyes blazing with anger.
'That monster has no rights over this innocent child.'

Gwenneth drew her brows together in puzzlement.

'You know nothing of the father.'

'I know that he is a rapist. That is all I need to know.'

'No, you've got it wrong. Epillicus didn't touch me.'

Valda shivered in disgust as she remembered the sweaty
hand that had slid all over her body that terrible night.

'I'm not talking about the Procurator's slave. I mean the
young Roman with the finger missing on his left hand.'

'But he didn't rape me.'

'Then how…' Valda gestured at the child smiling as he played with Gwenneth's curls.

'He loved me.'

'Then it was true…' Valda sank back onto the pile of furs.

'What was true?' asked Gwenneth impatiently. She was finding the conversation difficult to follow.

'He told me he loved you, but I didn't believe him.'

'Who told you?'

'The Roman with the missing finger. I met him after the battle.'

'What battle?' Gwenneth asked, more confused than ever.

'Of course. You left before it started.'

'What started? In the name of Camulos and all the gods, explain what you are talking about.'

'I'd better tell you from the beginning.'

'I think you should,' said Gwenneth.

***

The fire had died down to glowing embers before the story was told with Gwenneth having to interrupt time and time again to clarify a point on which Valda was vague or where she assumed knowledge her cousin didn't have. Talking for the first time about the rebellion and its aftermath helped Valda come to terms with the death of her sister and her part in her mother's death, but for Gwenneth, it brought more uncertainty. It emphasised the gulf between Marcus and herself. When the moment came for him to make a choice, he had abandoned her and fought against her people. Although he had sent Valda to her with a message to wait, she wondered whether in the end she could forgive him for what he had done. Maybe he had returned and had been searching for her ever since, but even if they should one day find each other again, she did not see there could be any future for them together despite the child they had made.

She tried to explain this feeling of hopelessness to Valda who had seemed excited by the thought that Gwenneth and

Marcus would one day be together. Valda took her cousin by the hand and looked into her eyes.

'I think the blame on both sides is equal. Before my father died, he was content to lead the Iceni as a subjugated people. Of course, there were injustices. Power and corruption are yoked together like a pair of oxen yoked to the plough, whoever cultivates the field. Men are either rulers or their subjects, and when rulers quarrel, the rest of us are trampled into the earth.'

She stopped speaking whilst she stirred the smouldering embers and added more logs to the hearth. Gwenneth waited for her to continue. The baby had fallen asleep. Once the fire was blazing, Valda began speaking again.

'Some rulers are worse than others. My mother was the worst of all. She wanted power, whatever the cost. She roused the tribes to fight a war they could not win. It did not matter to her how many people died, and in the end, I honestly think she had been driven mad by the need to kill. She left no one – man, woman or child – alive and not a building was left standing in the three towns she attacked.'

There was a silence between them when Valda finished speaking. Gwenneth stared at the flames and thought about what had been said. The issues of right and wrong, friendship and enmity seemed to be matters of individual choice. Marcus had left her, but he had not abandoned her. He had gone to do his duty as he saw it. He did not know about the child. In all that time, with everything that was happening, he had remembered her and sent Valda to find her with a message that he loved her. He had helped her cousin escape despite his allegiance to Rome and the glory that would have been his if he had taken her hostage.

What a mess it all was. She wondered what had been happening since Boudicca's death. The Roman army must be consolidating their position – that would explain the activity at the fort. But where was Marcus and how could she find him? She couldn't very well go to the fort and ask for him – they would think she was a spy and might kill her on the spot. Then it struck her. It would soon be a year to the day since they met.

Perhaps, he would remember too and come to look for her by the river again. It was a chance, though a small one, and the only one she really had. She turned to look at her cousin who was sitting quietly, waiting for her to work things out.

'Valda, I need to go and look for him by the river, but I can't take the baby. Will you look after him? I will only be gone three days.'

Valda nodded, 'Of course, I love him as though he were my own son. When will you go?'

'At first light.'

It was settled. For the first time in many moons, Gwenneth felt no older than her eighteen years. She was a girl again, and she was going to find her lover, the father of her child.

***

Marcus was worried. Time was running out. His work at the fort was nearly finished and the new governor, Publius Petronius Turpilianus, would be arriving soon. Since Paulinus had departed in semi-disgrace, the province had been under the control of Cerealis, the commander of the Ninth. Cerealis had done well for himself, thought Marcus. Instead of following orders to march to Londinium against Boudicca, he had stayed in the new fortress at Lindum. He had claimed that the northern defences needed to be maintained to prevent an uprising in Brigantia, although he knew full well that Carimandua, the Brigantian queen, was involved in an internal power struggle against her husband and was not foolish enough to take on Rome as well.

So, whilst the rest of the army, reinforced by troops from the Rhine, had taken the war into the rebel heartlands looting and murdering as they went, Cerealis had enjoyed a quiet winter and was exonerated from any blame for the current state of unrest in the province. All the blame was firmly placed on the outgoing governor, Paulinus, by the ex-slave, Polyclitus, who had been sent by Nero to investigate the uprising.

The investigation had been very thorough. Marcus had been interviewed himself and given a hard time because of his father's friendship with Paulinus. Polyclitus had been pretty scathing about his failure to stop the flogging and rapes which had ignited the rebellion. It was because of these two factors – his relationship with the ex-governor and his ineffectual handling of the transfer of power from Prasutagus – that Marcus felt nervous about his future in the province. But how could he go back to Rome? His heart was here now. Yet, he had searched everywhere for Gwenneth and she was nowhere to be found. Instead, in his travels, he had seen firsthand the devastation wreaked by his fellow soldiers.

One day towards the middle of summer, he had returned to Boudicca's stronghold, where he found just a handful of people were left in the once-thriving settlement. There was not a well-fed individual amongst them. Their clothes hung in tatters from skeletal bodies. Children with swollen bellies and spindly limbs sat listlessly on the grass outside the ruins of their homes. Once again, he felt ashamed to be Roman. He had no one to talk to about his feelings. His only friend, Quintus, was dead.

He left wondering what good it would do if he did find Gwenneth. Perhaps, she would see him as one of the enemy. Instead of looking into eyes glowing gold-green and soft with love, she would look at him with eyes as hard and cold as emeralds. He did not think he could bear it if she hated him. Perhaps, it would be better to take the next ship to Gaul, return to his family and forget all about her.

By the time he reached Durobrivae, he was thoroughly miserable. He went to his room and sat on the hard bed. From the belt at his waist, he detached a small pouch and emptied the contents into his hand. The lock of gold on his palm gleamed in the shafts of sunlight pouring in through the open window. He had cut it from her head whilst she lay sleeping on their last night together. At the time, it had seemed like a silly sentimental impulse but over the last year, he had looked at it often, bending to inhale the honey fragrance which still lingered on each shining hair. He had to see her again, whatever the outcome. The day after tomorrow, it would be exactly a year since they met. If she loved him, then she would re-member and return. It was his only hope. He put the lock of hair back in the pouch and lay back on the bed. That night, he dreamed he once again held Gwenneth in his arms.

Chapter 19

Catus sailed away to Gaul, afraid of the hatred he had un-
leashed by his greed which had roused the province to war.
                    Tacitus. Annals 32.14-15

Valda and the baby were still asleep when Gwenneth left the
farm at dawn. The air was crisp with the promise of fine
weather, and she enjoyed the feel of the closely cropped turf,
which gave a spring to her step as she set off across the pas-
tureland in the direction of Durobrivae. It did not take her long
to reach the edge of the scarp this time. Her body had recovered from the demands put on it by her pregnancy, and she
walked quickly even where the ground was uneven and the
ascent was steep. The river below her sparkled in the morning
sun and her heart pounded as she scrambled down the slope
into the valley. She slipped off her shoes and delighted in
coolness of the mud that squelched between her toes as she
walked along the bank. It was wonderful to feel so free.

When she reached the place that had, for a short time, been
her home, she took off the bag she carried on her back and
emptied its contents onto the ground. She had brought the
tools she needed with her so her preparations were easier this
time. By nightfall, a little shelter stood beneath the trees, made
of hurdles as before, and the enticing aroma of roasting trout
promised a tasty dinner as a reward for her hard work.

***

Marcus spent the day in a waking dream. Thoughts of
Gwenneth, images of her body, her eyes, her hair streamed
through his mind and the sound of her laughter and soft voice

echoed through the jingle of harness and ringing of metal on metal as the soldiers drilled outside his billet. He had no work to fill his time and no friends in the fort to distract him. He would have to leave as soon as the new orders came from Turpilianus. He lay on his bed and watched the shadows lengthen on the concrete floor as the sun sank lower in the sky. At last, he fell into a restless sleep.

***

Gwenneth woke early. This was it. By sunset, she would know whether Marcus truly loved her or whether she had just been a diversion, soon forgotten. She rose from her bed of sweet-smelling grasses and went outside. It was going to be another glorious day. She stripped off her clothes and let herself down into the river. It was numbingly cold. Then her limbs began to tingle. She climbed out onto the bank and stretched out on her back in the grass. The warmth of the sun was like a tender caress, and she shivered as she thought of the possibilities that lay ahead. She ran her fingers slowly across her stomach and up to her breasts. Her body had changed. Would he still want her?

She sat up abruptly. Thoughts like that were fruitless. A churning feeling in her belly reminded her she was hungry. She went again to the edge of the water and dipped her hands into the current. Today, the trout proved elusive. They wriggled through her outstretched fingers and swam to safety. Eventually, she gave up. She reached for her tunic, then she remembered she had intended to bring the clothes she was wearing when they first met. She wanted to weep with frustration. Everything was going wrong.

She slid back into the water and floated for a while allowing the current to carry her downstream. The river widened and she came to rest in a shallow pool, feeling more relaxed. She got to her feet and waded back to where she had come from. She stood knee-deep watching the fish swimming through the reeds, remembering the day they had met. The shrill call of a magpie broke her reverie and she looked up at the sky. The sun was already past its zenith. Was he ever going to come? She lifted her arms to release the tension in her shoulders and wondered whether she should give up and go back to the farm. Then she heard a twig snap behind her and felt a prickle in her spine.

***

Marcus had forced himself to wait until the sun was high before saddling his horse and leaving the billet. He wanted to gallop away but kept to a steady trot until he reached the ford. After crossing, he allowed his horse to canter. It needed some exercise now if, as he hoped, it would be tethered for some time later. He slowed to a walk when he reached the bend in the river just before the clearing he was heading for. Then he saw it. The shelter had been rebuilt. She must be here. He swung down from the saddle. His fingers fumbled as he tried to tie the reins to the nearest tree. He padded through the trees, hoping to surprise her. The sight that met his eyes was beyond everything he had ever hoped for.

She was standing with her back towards him, knee-deep in the swirling water. Her red-gold hair cascaded over her shoulders and down to her slender waist. Her head was thrown back and her arms uplifted as if to embrace the sun. Her skin gleamed like fine white marble. It was as if a precious statue had come to life – Venus rising from the waves.

Gwenneth swung around. Green eyes locked with brown and stillness hung between them. Marcus was the first to move. He strode, fully clothed into the water and she felt the rough linen of his tunic against her skin. She clasped her arms about his neck and their lips met. Somehow, they found themselves lying back on the bank, limbs entwined. He entered her quickly and she gasped as they both found the release they needed. They parted and lay for a moment breathing hard, then turned to each other again. Without words, they caressed each other, rediscovering the feel of each other's bodies until every nerve seemed exposed. Gwenneth pulled Marcus on top of her and he entered her again. She shuddered as all tension was released and a languorous warmth spread out from the centre of her body. Marcus groaned as he felt her sigh beneath him. Roused by the pulsing heat of her, he thrust harder until he too lay spent and satiated. Then they slept.

***

Marcus was the first to wake. He lay on his side, propped up on one arm, and watched Gwenneth as she slept. Her body seemed more rounded than he remembered. Her curves were fuller and her stomach less taut. This surprised him. With the province in the grip of famine, he had expected to find her thin and starving. She was even more desirable than before, if that were possible. Where had she been all this time? Her hands were hard and calloused. Perhaps she had been working as a servant or captured as a slave. Here eyelids were smudged purple and her lashes cast a shadow that merged with the dark circles underneath her eyes and there were two little lines etched between her brows. Life must have been hard for her in the time they had been apart.

He felt a rush of love and drew her close. She stirred and their eyes met. He kissed her tenderly and drew back to look at her propped on his elbow again. To both of them, it was like looking at someone endearingly familiar but yet a stranger.

For the first time, Gwenneth noticed his eyes were not truly brown. When he smiled, as he was smiling now, chips of blue-like sapphires sparkled around the edge of the iris. She saw his beard was starting to grow and gently drew her fingers along the edge of his jaw enjoying the roughness of the stubble then testing the softness of his lips. She smiled as he nibbled her fingers and he, in turn, traced the dimples at the corner of her mouth. For a long time, neither of them felt the need to speak.

At last, he turned onto his back and looked at the sky. 'You had gone when I returned. There was nothing to show you were coming back. All traces of the shelter had gone.' His voice was sad as he remembered the way he had felt that day.

'I thought you had abandoned me,' she said, and her voice was flat and empty as the sky above them.

'I sent Valda to find you, to tell you I love you. Poor girl. She must have been caught or injured.' He didn't like to say to Gwenneth that anything worse had happened to her cousin, but he was afraid she must be dead.

'Valda did find me – or rather, I found her. I did go away, but I came back because every instinct told me you wouldn't leave me. She was trying to survive here on her own.'

'But didn't she give you my message or explain what had kept me from you?' Marcus asked, turning to look at her.

'Valda had lost her mind. She told me nothing until the day before yesterday. She thought you had raped me and were tricking her.'

'So, where did you go? Where have you been through this terrible winter? I searched everywhere. I even braved Boudicca's old stronghold.'

'I found a farm about ten miles from here. It had been deserted, so we have been tending the animals and working the land.'

'And I have been at the fort,' he said in wonder. 'Did you ever venture out from the farm? You know, I once thought I caught sight of you in the woods on the edge of the scarp when I was riding out on one of my fruitless searches. I caught a glimpse of a woman with hair the same colour as yours collecting wood last autumn. Then I realised she was much fatter and older. She could hardly walk she was so fat. Waddling she was, like this.'

He had jumped up and was listing from side to side, sure she would be amused at him being so silly to mistake her for a fat old woman. His comic turn was met with a stony silence. He stopped his fooling and looked down at her. Her mouth was set in a grim line and her eyes were emerald-cold. She stood up and put her tunic on, tying her girdle without a word. He was too stunned to move at first, but when she started to walk away, he caught hold of her elbow and tried to pull her back. She tore herself free and began to run. She reached the trees before Marcus caught up with her. They fell to the ground in a tangle of legs and arms. He sat astride her trying to get a hold of the clenched fists which flailed at his face. Her nails raked his neck leaving deep grooves in the flesh.

'That was me,' she sobbed when he had her wrists pinned to the ground. 'I was bearing your son and bent double with the first pains of labour. I hate you.' She spat in his face then tears spilled down her cheeks as she remembered that day and the hope she had felt when she saw the rider on the skyline. He had abandoned her not once but twice.

Marcus was stunned. Now he understood the changes in her body. She had borne him a son. He was filled with wonder. Pity and love overwhelmed him. He released her wrists and gathered her into his lap, stroking her hair away from her forehead as he muttered gentle words of comfort as if to a child, until the sobs ceased and she lay quietly in his arms.

Gwenneth was surprised by her own reaction. She had not realised how bitter she felt. The months of worry and uncertainty had affected her more than she knew. She had meant to tell him he had a son when the moment was right, not fling it in his face like an accusation. She looked up at him, her lips trembling, her eyes glistening with unshed tears.

He smiled back but his face was stern. 'What have you done with my son?'

She saw the fear in his face and was quick to reassure him.

'He is safe at the farm with Valda.'

His face reddened with anger and he spoke with an effort, trying not to lose control. 'How could you? You said she was mad.'

'Not any longer. The madness left her as her love grew for our son. She is like a second mother to him. I would have brought him with me but my milk has dried. Valda feeds him with the milk of a nursing ewe. She saved his life.'

Marcus nodded. It had happened to his mother too, and he had often been told the story when he was a boy of how his life had been saved when he was a baby by the milk of one of their goats. He had been given the very feeding bottle his mother had used as soon as he was old enough to understand what it meant.

'What is he like, this son of mine?'

'Luckily, he favours his mother,' she said with a smile, running her thumb over the arch of his nose.

Marcus laughed, 'When does Valda expect you back?'

'Not until tomorrow.' Gwenneth's smile broadened.

He picked her up and took her back into the shelter. Night fell unnoticed and the first birds were calling when they fell into a heavy satiated sleep.

Chapter 20

*Britain is the biggest island we know. It stretches from a
point opposite Germany to a point opposite Spain and the
southern coast is visible from France. There is no more land
to the north.*

Tacitus. Agricola X

It was noon before Marcus and Gwenneth left the shelter the
next day. Whilst dressing and eating the remains of the provisions Marcus had brought with him, they talked easily about
what they had done over the months of their separation.

Gwenneth saw her lover was impressed at the way she had
coped at the farm, firstly on her own and pregnant and then
with just Valda, whose mind had been unbalanced by her experiences, until the baby was born when there was another to
take care of.

She listened in horror as Marcus described how the province had been devastated by the rebellion and its aftermath
and the destitution facing many of her people. She realised
how lucky she had been to find a refuge and understood now
why the farmer, her kinsman Bodwyn, had not returned to
claim his land and home. She grieved at so many lives lost
and ruined because of one woman's lust for revenge – or was
it really the lust for power which had driven her? They would
never know. It was a mercy Boudicca was dead, but what
would become of the Iceni now?

Gwenneth saw that Marcus was curious to know how she
had found the farm, as it was so well-hidden and he had never
found it when he was searching for her. She told him about
her visit to Eisu in search of her brother and how it was from
him, she learned her mission was pointless and from him, she

had learned of the whereabouts of the farm as a place to stay overnight on the way back home. It was on that journey she had found him in the ditch. They both looked down at his hand at the same moment. She turned away with tears in her eyes.

Marcus realised that she still thought herself cursed. Well, she needn't be afraid any longer, he thought. He launched into an account of the battle on the shores of Holy Island, the destruction of the sacred groves and the end of the druid's power.

Gwenneth listened spellbound and when his story was told, felt relief running through her like a cleansing stream. She had been so worried about the future. It had been hard enough for the two women to grow and make enough for their own needs, especially with the child to look after, so building up a surplus of grain or livestock to trade for the essentials they couldn't grow themselves or make, like iron tools and salt, would have been impossible. Even though the farm was well-hidden, eventually, the Roman tax officials would have stumbled across them. Then there was their son. He would need friend and companions of his own age. As she and Valda grew older, they would have become weak and unable to work. If she could once again be part of the tribe her kinsmen could help her.

She dared not think of what would happen to Marcus. He was a Roman and had been sent to her homeland for a purpose. Now that his job was over, he would be sent somewhere else. The best she could hope for was for him to stay in touch and maybe help them with gifts of money. Visiting would be next to impossible. Well, she would enjoy whatever time was left to them. Every memory must be a happy one to sustain her in the lonely years ahead.

Marcus went to fetch his horse and Gwenneth packed away the few things she had brought with her. She looked at the shelter. Should she leave it standing? She was still hesitating when he returned. He understood immediately what was in her mind.

'Leave it. I would like to think it was still here, even if we are not.'

She smiled in agreement, glad that he felt that way. He helped her into the saddle and mounted behind her.

'Let's go and see our son.'

***

The shadows were lengthening when Valda heard the thud of hooves. She swiftly took up the sleeping baby from his crib and gently placed him amongst a pile of furs in the sleeping bay. Then she took up an iron bar from the side of the hearth and hid it in the fold of her dress. The lovers entered side by side. Gwenneth saw the empty crib and the colour drained from her face. Marcus looked at her and then followed the direction of her gaze. In two strides, he reached Valda and grabbed her by the throat.

'What have you done with him?' he snarled.

She tried to speak, but he was choking the life out of her. The iron bar fell from her hand. Gwenneth understood then why the crib was empty. The baby would be hidden some-where safe. She grabbed Marcus from behind, pulling at his arms, trying to loosen his grip, but in his fear for his son, he had lost all control. Gwenneth despaired of making him see reason then a shrill cry came from the depths of the hut. The baby had woken up in the dark surrounded by unfamiliar tex-tures and smells and screamed in protest. The noise brought Marcus to his senses. He released Valda and she collapsed on the ground. Appalled by his lack of control, he knelt down beside her full of remorse, mumbling apologies. She sat up rubbing her throat and smiled at him.

Seeing that Valda did not seem to bear Marcus any ill will for his rough treatment, Gwenneth went to collect the baby. He stopped crying immediately and beamed at his mother. She took him over to his father and the two stared curiously at each other.

'What is his name?'

Gwenneth looked at Valda and said, 'In our tribe, it is a custom for the father to name the child.'

Marcus, seeing the exchange of glances, realised the importance of this moment. He thought very carefully before he spoke again.

'Then the child shall have three names, according to the custom of my people. His family name will be Saturninus. That is my family name and my father's family name and the family name of our ancestors. In this way, I acknowledge him as my son.'

This was far more than Gwenneth had hoped for.

'Next, I name him Quintus. Quintus was a friend of mine and he died for his country. If my son is like Quintus, he will be a good man. Finally, I name him Mardunad, in honour of your kinswoman who died tragically for her country. Mardunad and Quintus fought on different sides, but in this naming, they are joined, just as our people do in the birth of my son.'

Gwenneth felt a great sense of peace. A child's name was the first gift a father gave his son, and in his choice, Marcus had showed wisdom and compassion.

Young Quintus was unmoved by the solemnity of the occasion. He was hungry and started to bawl. Marcus hastily handed him over to Valda who rocked him gently whilst Gwenneth set about preparing the milk.

Whilst the two women attended to the baby, Marcus looked around the hut. It was only the second time he had been inside a native dwelling and this was quite different from Boudicca's palace. The first thing that struck him was how gloomy it was. The only source of natural light apart from the door was a hole in the roof. Torches supplemented the glow from the fire on the central hearth, but the periphery of the room was almost completely dark. This was a far cry from the light and airy rooms in his family home. It was also strange to be in a circular building. There was very little furniture but even so, the living space seemed cramped. He guessed that the curtained off areas were used for sleeping. He wondered how they kept themselves clean. Bathing was something he was used to doing every day.

As the women were still busy with the baby, he went outside. The sun cast a ruddy glow over the fields. He could hear the cattle lowing, and sheep were dotted over the valley slopes. The peaceful scene stirred a feeling of longing for the estates of his father's farm. He imagined a villa standing at the top of the rise, built of stone with a red-tiled roof, rooms enclosing a central courtyard in which a fountain spouted clear water brought by pipes from the nearby stream, a bathhouse at one end, heated with an underground furnace, with mosaic floors and walls decorated with beautiful pictures inspired by mythology and nature. The fields around the villa would be golden with ripening corn and a great barn would replace this hut, empty but waiting for the harvest.

At last, he knew what he wanted. He no longer yearned to be a soldier, dying as Quintus had in a country far away from his home, or bringing death and destruction to the people his empire had conquered, like Cerealis. He did not want to be a public official, like Decianus, caught up in the petty details of administration, or a politician, like Classicianus, dealing in lies and intrigue. He wanted to be a farmer, like his father, out in the fresh air, feeling the sun on his face and the earth beneath his feet, not in his own land but here in Britannia. This was where he wanted to stay, with Gwenneth and his son, watching the seasons change as the years rolled by.

The sun had disappeared below the horizon when Gwenneth came out to look for him. He put his arms around her shoulders and drew her close. Tomorrow, he would tell her of his dream. For the moment, it was enough they had found each other again.

Chapter 21

Bees hummed amongst the flowers and an exotic fragrance hung in the warm air. Gwenneth closed her eyes. It was pleasant to sit out in the courtyard at this time of year. The gentle splashing of water on stone was making her fell sleepy.

She awoke with a start. Shrill voices shattered the peace of the afternoon. She sighed. Young Quintus was fighting with his sister again. She wondered what had started them off this time. They used to get on so well. Wearily, she struggled to rise. Her bulk was making even walking uncomfortable. A calm voice rose above the shrieking and the quarrelling stopped in an instant. Thankfully, she settled back amongst the cushions. Valda was so good with the children. It was lucky she had come to visit now. Her work with the Council was very demanding and she rarely had time to get away. Gwenneth had reached the stage in her pregnancy when even the slightest exertion exhausted her and the friction between Quintus and Calpurnia drove her to distraction. Looking back at her own relationship with Corin, she could see similarities in the way their relationship deteriorated as they approached adolescence. If her own children followed the same path, they would become close friends again but it was going to be difficult for a couple of years more at least. She would be glad when this baby was born and she regained her old energy. Really though, her life was easy enough now. Her thoughts drifted back to the days when she had worked from dawn to dusk when she was carrying Quintus.

Ten years had passed since that terrible summer when Boudicca had led the tribes in revolt. Four emperors had come and gone and the Roman world had been split by civil war.

Vespasian had emerged as victor and the empire had not crumbled, as everyone had predicted.

She knew Marcus thought that the new Emperor would be sympathetic to Britannia, mainly because he had served with the Second at the time of the conquest. Gwenneth wasn't sure why this would make him favour this province over any other. Rather, she thought, the opposite would be true. She kept her thoughts to herself. She and Marcus did not always see eye to eye on politics. In the Brigantian affair last year, Marcus had argued passionately for Queen Carimandua whereas she had supported the consort, Venutius, who had been a hero of hers when she was younger. The governor had been of the same opinion as Marcus and sent a force to try and restore the queen. Fortunately, the fighting had not spread down south, but the rebellion wasn't put down until Vespasian sent yet another new governor to deal with it. His name was Cerealis. Apparently, he too had served in the army in Britain commanding the Ninth. Marcus said he knew him but cut her off when she started to ask questions. She had held her tongue, remembering that his friend Quintus had served in that legion.

Cerealis was having more success than his predecessors. Venutius was on the run and there was talk of extending the province right up into Caledonia. Gwenneth didn't mind what the politicians did as long as she and her family were left in peace.

It had been a struggle, but now their farm was a prosperous estate. This was all down to Marcus. He had seen the potential in the farm that had once belonged to Bodwyn. Soon after they had met again, he had travelled to Londinium to see the new procurator, Classicianus. He had come back with documents signing Bodwyn's land to him and his heirs in perpetuity. Gwenneth had been angry at first, not wanting to cheat a kinsman, but Marcus had persuaded her that it was the right thing to do as anyone who thought they had a claim to the land had two years in which to come forward. She was secretly relieved when the two years were up and there had been no counter claim. In addition, Marcus had entered into a contract to supply the forts at Lindum and Durobrivae with corn for the next five years. To Gwenneth's surprise, his father was extremely supportive of Marcus in this enterprise and had offered financial help until the estate was well established.

Marcus had worked tirelessly to achieve his ambition. His vision had carried them through the first few difficult years. He had planted and harvested every available acre and taken on men and women who had lost their land and possessions during the revolt to help him. A series of very fine summers and his own unflagging effort had produced record yields. Although Gwenneth was soon carrying Calpurnia, she had added her effort to this, although Marcus had been uneasy at first.

Valda had stayed with them for a while, taking responsibility for the livestock, which grazed the land where corn would not grow, and to continue caring for Quintus, but when Calpurnia was two, she left them to take up a position on the new Council established in Camulodunum. As she was the sole surviving member of the Icenian royal family, she thought it her duty to help her countrymen and get the region back on its feet. She soon gained a reputation for wisdom and justice and became her people's champion. Although Gwenneth missed her daily companionship, she was glad she had found something to do that suited her so well. They met sometimes when Marcus took Gwenneth with him to town when he went on business. Valda never married. All her love was invested in Quintus and Calpurnia.

There had been another baby. Sadly, she had not lived long enough to have a name. The tiny body lay beneath the corner of the fine house Marcus had built in their third year on the farm. Gwenneth had thought she would never be able to bear another child. The promise of a fourth, after so many years, seemed like a special gift from the gods.

Fortune had certainly smiled on them. Marcus had met the terms of his contract with the army and negotiated a lucrative second deal. The house he had dreamed of had been completed in two seasons. Gwenneth missed the hut which had been demolished to make way for a huge granary. She knew her attachment was purely sentimental. As Marcus said, it had been dark and stuffy but, despite the underfloor heating her husband was so proud of, sometimes she felt the rooms in the new house were cold and rather bare.

His latest idea was to add a bath suite. She did not really see the need for such extravagance. There was a stream nearby and they still used the old well. She occasionally visited the public baths when they went to town but it was to please Marcus, not for her own enjoyment. She found the idea of sitting in a pool of warm water with a lot of other women rather immodest and less hygienic that the stream. It was strange to think her own children would grow up taking such customs for granted and the old ways would be forgotten. She wondered what Corin would make of it all.

She found herself thinking about Corin a lot these days. In ten years, there had been no word from him. Wherever Marcus travelled, he made enquiries, but he always shook his head when she looked at him with the unspoken question in her eyes on his return.

She tried to make herself more comfortable on the couch. It was nearly time to eat. Marcus should be back in time for them to dine together. He had been gone three days, and she and Valda had prepared all his favourite dishes – the pies and puddings he loved but she found rather indigestible. It was a pity, but he was not a great meat eater.

Two strong arms seized her from behind. She felt a rush of tenderness as she looked down at the seven fingers spread across her swollen belly and shivered with pleasure as her husband pressed his lips against the nape of her neck. It was always like this when they met, even after the shortest of separations. Their bodies never seemed to tire of each other. She had thought when she was carrying Calpurnia, he would find her size and ungainliness unattractive but he did not seem to notice that she was clumsy and awkward, only that her eyes shone and her face glowed. It was the same now. Once, when they had just made love shortly before Calpurnia was born, and he was whispering how much he adored her, she reminded him of the time he had not recognised her because she was big with Quintus. He had been indignant, accusing her of making it up and swearing that he would always know and love her.

She had not pressed the matter further, but she remembered and was glad that he loved her so much he could not imagine a time when she had not filled him with desire.

Marcus came around to kneel in front of her. He looked up, his brown eyes glinting with those little chips of sapphire that told her he was laughing inside.

'I have found some at last.'

For a moment, she couldn't think what he meant. Then she remembered. The Arretine goblets that Quintus had brought with him from Rome so many years ago. Marcus had been searching for years, first of all to try and find the very pair his friend had owned, then when he realised they were lost forever, to try and find exact replicas. To him, they had become a symbol that linked the past to the future. He had been drinking from one of the pair when he had first seen her and noticed them in the old soldier's room at Durobrivae on his visit to the fort after Boudicca was flogged, her daughters raped and she had been branded. Although she would never really forget the horrors of that day, it was the first time they had kissed.

'Tonight, we will fill them with the very best Falernian wine and raise a toast to my old friend.'

***

Gerry woke with a start to find the hostel warden standing in front of her. She had fallen asleep in the hostel courtyard after breakfast

'Sorry to wake you,' he said, 'but are you here for another night? I have to get on and clean the room if you're not.'

'No problem,' replied Gerry. 'I'm not staying so I'll collect my things and be off.'

The warden left her to get on with her routine and Gerry hurried upstairs. Twenty minutes later, she walked through the gate onto the site.

Peter must have been looking out for her because he was out of his caravan before she got to her tent and almost ran to catch up with her. He took her in his arms and kissed her lightly. She pulled away quickly looking around to see if anyone was watching them.

'Tom and Annie have already figured out we're sleeping together,' he said, 'and no one else can see us from the trench.'

He bent to kiss her again and this time she responded. It felt good to be back in his arms.

'That's enough for now,' he said at last. 'Dump your stuff and grab some tools. I want to examine another part of the site and have been waiting for you to get started.'

Gerry joined Peter at the side of the trench a few minutes later, carefully avoiding looking at the walls of the excavated building, although she had noticed as she passed there was a newly dug hole at the corner.

'I want you to trowel over the area over there,' he said.

She was glad to see he was pointing to the bottom of the slope about fifty metres away from where they stood. Although telling Peter of her loss had been cathartic, she would have hated to be working so close to a place that was witness to a similar tragedy, even though it happened more than two thousand years ago.

'What are you hoping to find?' Gerry asked.

'I want to see if there were any other structures associated with the building we've found or, even better, which may have pre-dated it.'

'So, you hope there might be an Iron Age hut?'

'Clever girl,' he said and she winced a little at the hint of patronage.

He caught her expression.

'Sorry,' he said. 'There I go again underestimating your knowledge and intelligence. Yes, I'm looking for some evidence of continuity to show that the Brits adopted the Roman way of life even this early on and in this particular area where there was so much unrest.'

He kissed her again and left her to it.

Gerry enjoyed the satisfaction of removing the last traces of earth from the underlying limestone to reveal what appeared to be random circles and lines of dark earth that stood out starkly against the dazzling white of the bedrock. When she reached the side of the trench, she stood up to check her handiwork. A long shadow fell across the ground in front of her. She looked up and recognized Peter's silhouette against the deep blue sky. Her heart gave an odd little leap and she felt her stomach contract. She had forgotten her earlier irritation.

He jumped down to stand beside her and took her hand. She pulled it away quickly. He laughed. 'You're right, there'll be plenty of time for that later.' He looked across the area she had just trowelled. 'What an excellent job you have made of cleaning this up. Look what you've revealed.' He took her hand again and led her to the middle of the trench. He pointed to a perfect circle of tiny holes outlined by four curving lines.

'If I'm not mistaken, this is just what I was hoping to find. Here we have the drip gully from the conical thatched roof of an iron age round house and these little holes are the stake holes from the wattle fence that formed the walls. Stake holes don't usually show up as well as this. Only the very best trowellers can make them so distinct.'

Gerry felt herself blushing with pleasure at his praise. She looked again and saw the pattern clearly for herself. Then she noticed eight much larger circles, four in the middle of what Peter seemed to think was a house but the other four arranged in a square, off to the side.

'Those larger holes look like they held posts,' she said, 'but why aren't they all inside the house?'

'I was wondering that myself,' he said, taking his trowel out of his back pocket and crouching down next to the nearest offset circle which seemed to be right on top of the curved gully. He scraped gently. 'Look, can you see a slight difference in colour?'

Gerry saw that there was indeed a more orange look to the soil in the circular hole than in the gully.

Peter probed a little further. 'It looks like the posts were driven into the ground after the round house went out of use,' he said his voice rising in pitch with excitement and his accent becoming more noticeable. 'These offset holes are cutting through the four holes that would have held the posts that supported the roof of the roundhouse. I think they belong to another structure entirely. The only four post structures I am aware of belong to granaries. So, I can see a sequence here – an Iron Age farm becomes a Roman villa and the original hut is demolished and replaced with a granary. We have our evidence for continuity!'

'Not necessarily,' said Gerry. 'How did an Icenian farmer, just after the rebellion, get rich enough to replace his hut with a stone building and have enough surplus grain to make it worthwhile building a granary?'

'Maybe he collaborated with the Romans and this was his reward,' said Peter.

'Or maybe, the land was stolen from one of the rebels and given to a Roman soldier,' said Gerry, 'although it would be an odd gift and a very brave Roman who would want to live so far away from established centres when the unrest was so recent.'

This is one of the questions archaeology can't resolve, Gerry thought sadly. They would never know who really lived here.

***

That evening, Peter took Gerry down to the village for a meal to celebrate. They sat side by side on one of the padded benches waiting for their order to arrive. The pub was empty as it was still early and a weekday night and they were out of sight of the bored barmaid in a little alcove next to the inglenook so there was no one to see them acting like lovesick teenagers.

The clatter of high heels on the flagged floor announced the arrival of their food, and Peter let go of Gerry's fingers and passed her one of the sets of cutlery the waitress had unloaded from the tray along with two bowls of steaming soup.

'I've finally placed your accent,' said Gerry as she unrolled the paper napkin and extracted a spoon.

'My accent? I didn't think I had one anymore,' said Peter in surprise.

'It's only really noticeable when you're excited,' said Gerry.

'Well, that must be all the time I'm talking to you,' he said with a smile.

She smiled reluctantly. He was rather too keen on double entendres.

'Well, out with it then,' he said. 'What accent do you think I have?'

'Italian,' she replied.

'Si, esatto. You're exactly right. I was brought up in the countryside just outside Rome but my family moved to England when I was a teenager.'

'Then you're a Roman and I'm a native from Norfolk. If we'd here lived two thousand years ago, we would have been enemies,' said Gerry.

'Luckily, we didn't,' Peter replied.

Chapter 22

Gerry was working at the end of the trench furthest away from the caravans and tents. The walls of the villa had been removed and the postholes emptied. Annie was in the marquee washing the last pieces of pottery and bone. The volunteers had left that morning and the geophysicists were packing up their equipment and loading the lorry for the first trip back to the depot. Peter had gone with Anthony up to Warham Camp for one last dowsing session as their last one had been cut short by Gerry's discovery of the infant skeleton. Tom was drawing a plan of the hut. The site was quiet and peaceful.

Tom and Peter had had an animated discussion that morning over breakfast about whether the surface Gerry was now working on was the natural limestone. It was crumblier than elsewhere on the site. Peter thought that it was just a geological difference in the rock, which is why he hadn't wanted much time spent on it. Tom was convinced that sometime in the past, it had been open ground and the texture was due to weathering, which meant there might be more to find. Peter had said that he hoped not as it was the penultimate day of the excavation and the JCB was booked to come and backfill the trench in two days' time, but he agreed that they should take a look anyway for the sake of completeness.

Gerry smiled as she remembered their conversation. It had been good humoured, but Tom had been quietly insistent in the face of his boss's conviction. In the end, he had persuaded Peter by citing good practice, reminding him that it was their responsibility to ensure that every avenue was explored in the interests of research. It did Peter good to be challenged, she thought. He could be a bit overbearing sometimes. Her smile changed to a frown. Perhaps, this didn't bode well for what might happen to them as an item after the dig ended. They hadn't talked about the future at all. He would go back to his job in London but she had nothing planned. This dig had been fun, but it wasn't going to help her career.

She sat back on her heels and looked at the area she had been trowelling. Tom had suggested she take a couple of inches off the surface to see if anything showed up. It was hard work and her wrists were aching. She couldn't see any change. Still, she was more than half way across the trench and should be finished by tea break.

It had been overcast all morning, but now the sun was coming out. She stripped off her jumper and threw it up onto the baulk then bent back over her work. The repetitive actions – scraping off the loose chips of limestone, scooping them up into her shovel, tipping the shovel into the bucket and empty-ing the bucket into the wheelbarrow – allowed her mind to roam freely. She deliberately blocked any worries about the future and wondered instead about the people who had once lived here. The tragedy of a stillbirth made her feel a direct connection to the family that must have occupied the villa. Was it the same family that once lived in the hut?

She was so absorbed in dreaming about the past that she didn't immediately register how much easier it was getting to use her trowel. A faint chink of metal against metal brought her back to the present, and she saw the gleam of silver as a circular object sprung out of the ground and arched through the air. It hit her bucket and fell on the ground in front of her. She quickly stuck her trowel in the place where it had come from and called to Tom. Hearing the excitement in her voice, he put down the board which he was using to draw on and came over to join her.

'Look,' she said, pointing with a shaking hand. 'I think I've found a coin.'

'You most certainly have,' he said as he knelt beside her and bent over to take a closer look. It had landed heads up. He peered intently at the image. 'I think it might be Flavian,' he said softly. 'You know what that means. Whatever is under-neath could be around the turn of the century.'

'But will we find anything underneath?' Gerry asked. 'I thought I was this was just an old land surface.'

'You've already found it,' said Tom, standing up. 'See this darker soil mixed in with the limestone? I think it's the fill of a pit or something.'

Gerry stood up too to get a better view and at the same time, the sun disappeared behind a cloud. Without the glare, the contrast in colour was much easier to see.

'I thought I felt a difference!' she exclaimed.

'I'll get the theodolite to measure in the coordinates for the coin – thank goodness it wasn't on the first lorry trip back to the depot. You go and tell Annie and get a plastic bag. Then I think we'll stop for tea.'

***

After the break, Gerry was eager to get back to the trench. Her task, which had seemed a bit pointless before, had a real purpose now. She worked fast to define the edge of the looser material and was puzzled to find there seemed to be a firmer bit in the centre. She was expecting this to be round like some of the other pits they had found the previous week, which Peter had interpreted as underground granaries, and probably belonging to the iron age period of occupation. The date would have been a bit late though if Tom's guess about the coin was right. She got to the other side of the trench and looked back at what she had done. It wasn't one round pit she had found but two oblong ones. These weren't pits though. The shape was unmistakeable. It was two graves!

'I have a sense of deja vu,' said Tom as he stood beside Gerry yet again looking at the surface she'd trowelled. 'Looks like I'm going to have to go down the village to phone Peter. Luckily, the Home Office licence covers us for exhumation until the end of the dig, but he'll need to get Sue, the osteoarchaeologist back to record and lift the bones – it was her who lifted the neonatal bones. You can make a start on removing the fill whilst I'm gone. Take it carefully down in spits – I would suggest five to ten centimetres at a time. Stop when you can see the top of the cranium. As you know, that should be the first thing you come across.'

'Which one should I do first?' asked Gerry. 'Or would you like me to work on them both?'

'I think it would be better if you do one at a time,' said Tom after a moment's thought. 'Hopefully, I should be back by the time you have got to that stage with both of them.'

'Do you want me to sieve the excavated material in case?' Gerry asked.

'No,' replied Tom. 'There's no sign of any animal or root disturbance, so all the bones should be in place. Sieving can wait until we have found the skulls.'

By the time Tom returned from the village, Gerry had exposed a small disc of yellow in each grave and was sitting cross-legged on the baulk, her feet well away from the edge to prevent it collapsing. She had emptied the wheelbarrow and collected a sieve from the tool shed ready for the second stage.

'Great job,' said Tom. 'You've kept the surface nice and even and haven't gone too far down.'

'It was really easy to tell when I was close,' said Gerry.

'Yes, there's a real difference in the feel of the earth where it touches the bone, isn't there? I managed to get through to Peter and he's going to collect Sue and bring her back to the site tomorrow morning. I've brought over a leaf trowel and brushes for us both and another bucket for me. I'll take the one on the far side and you can have the one nearest the trench edge. We can share your barrow.'

They both began uncovering the skeletons, working methodically from head to neck to torso to arms and legs, to hands and feet, first squatting to the side, then lying on the ground to reach into the graves as they went deeper so they didn't trample on the remains. They took off only enough soil to be able to see the outlines of the long bones and the position of the hands and feet, leaving the removal of the rest for when Sue was present.

They didn't finish until the light was fading. Annie had prepared supper for the three of them. They were all tired and went to bed soon after they had finished eating. Gerry had spent every night over the past two weeks in Peter's caravan, so at first, it felt odd to sleep into her own tent – odd but strangely pleasant. She was aching from the unaccustomed positions she had been forced to adopt to avoid stepping on the bones, so having the space to move about freely was great – it was warm enough not to have to get inside the sleeping bag. Like a lot of men, she had known Peter was particular about the side he slept on, which in his case was the outside, so she had been pinned up against the caravan wall – though that was marginally better than being pushed out of the bed altogether. She wondered again what the future might hold. They had been passionate lovers, but she sensed his interest was beginning to wane. Examining her feelings, she realised that her own attraction was fading too. She remembered her first impression of his character, as opposed to his body, had not been great. There was definitely a chemistry between there which served them well in bed but as she knew from her own bitter experience, more was needed to sustain a lasting relationship. To put it frankly, he was just a little bit too full of himself. Well, there was only one more day and one more night before she headed home. Tom and Annie had already promised her a lift back to Oxford. There was no need to rock the boat. They would be busy lifting the skeletons tomorrow and would be bound to have an end of dig drink or two in the evening, so sex was probably off the menu anyway if that first night together was anything to go by.

***

The Land Rover drew up just as Gerry was finishing her second cup of coffee outside the mess caravan. A tall woman with a head of stunning white hair got out of the passenger side and walked over to join her.

'Hi,' she said with a smile which lit up her blue eyes. 'You must be Gerry. I'm Sue, the osteoarchaeologist. We missed each other last time I was here.'

Gerry smiled back. 'Yes, that's me. I had to go to the village that morning,' she said, her voice carefully neutral, although the anguish of the discovery was no longer acute. 'Would you like a coffee?'

Sue nodded. 'Yes, please. It's a long drive up from Colchester and we had to get up early this morning. I expect Peter would like one too. He's just gone to get the post from the village. He'll be back in a few minutes.'

Gerry went inside and came back with two steaming mugs. She handed one to Sue and put the other on the table. After her musings the night before, she was glad she didn't have to meet Peter just yet.

'Shall we go over to have a look at what you've found?' said Sue as Gerry drained her mug. 'I can take my coffee with me, and you can leave Peter's here.'

***

They had covered the area with tarpaulins when they finished drawing and photographing the graves and their contents the day before, more as a gesture of respect than a defence against the weather. There hadn't been any rain forecast. Tom had already taken the coverings off when Sue and Gerry arrived. He had a stack of plastic bags and boxes ready to put the bones in and some pro forma sheets with a skeleton drawn on so they could check which bones were present.

Gerry found that the work of dismantling the skeletons was almost as satisfying as uncovering them. She and Tom took one grave each. As they lifted each bone from the earth, Sue ticked it off on the sheet and told them the correct medical names. They started with the skulls and worked down the body just as they had when they were taking the earth away. As the graves were gradually emptied, Gerry found she could work from inside rather than bent over and leaning in from the top surface, so it was much quicker and infinitely more comfortable. Just as well, as her muscles were achingly stiff from the day before. She had reached the hands and started with the right. This was the fiddliest part of the work as there were a lot of very small bones.

'Well done.' said Sue. 'You've got every single one, even the wrist bones and the tips of the fingers.'

Gerry put them all together in a single plastic bag and moved over to start on the left hand. She saw immediately there was something wrong. 'Oh no, I seem to have hacked out one of the fingers.'

Sue got down on her knees and peered over the edge. 'So you have. How odd. It must be somewhere in the soil that's left in the grave. Otherwise, you would have found it yesterday whilst you were sieving. Never mind. I expect we'll find it later when the remaining soil is sieved. Don't worry. These things happen.'

Gerry was annoyed with herself. She had been so careful yesterday when she was taking the fill away from the bones. She put the remaining phalanges into a new plastic bag then started picking up the metatarsals, the bones that supported them. The one in the middle looked bit odd. She held it up to Sue.

'Look this one has a funny end.'

Sue took the slender fragment from Gerry. 'So, it has,' she said. She examined it closely.

'That's strange! It's actually been sawn. See this surface here, it's completely flat and shiny. I've never seen anything like it. Why on earth would anyone saw off a middle finger? I'll have fun looking at this under the microscope.'

***

Once the skeletons were safely stowed away in boxes and loaded into the Land Rover, Gerry made coffee for herself and Sue. They had left Tom to remove the soil that was left in the two graves. Peter and Anthony had gone off to Warham Camp with the geophysicists and Annie was clearing up in the marquee. The two women sat on the bench outside the mess caravan in companionable silence enjoying the warmth of the late morning sun. The shared experience of working on the bones had made them easy with each other. It was Sue who spoke first.

'Peter was telling me on the way here that you were hoping to take up archaeology as a career.'

Gerry's immediate reaction was anger that her personal ambitions had been the subject of a casual conversation to pass the time on a long journey. She turned her face away and stared into the distance.

'Don't be cross,' said Sue, reaching out to touch Gerry's wrist. 'Peter and I have been colleagues for a long time and there was a very good reason he told me about you. You see, I have managed to get a grant to pay for someone to work with me for six months on a new project to see what teeth can tell us about where someone came from. The pay is rubbish and the timing doesn't work for anyone looking to do a PhD so I haven't been able to recruit. Peter thought you might be interested. I was watching you as we worked together and I can see you're careful and methodical and we seem to get on OK. It may not sound much of a career opportunity, but I can promise you a research paper out of it and it is an interesting and innovative field. What do you say?'

Gerry was stunned. Her anger had dissipated whilst Sue was speaking. So, Peter had been thinking of the future, after all. OK, not their shared future but actually this was far better.

Sue mistook her silence for reluctance. 'I'm sorry. Was I being patronising? I really would like to work with you but you probably have all sorts of offers in the pipeline.'

'No, no, I would love to,' said Gerry. 'Tell me more.'

A shout from Tom interrupted them, 'Hey, come over here and bring Annie.'

The three women hurried over to the far side of the trench.

'Look, what I've found,' said Tom. He pointed to the bottom of the grave where a glossy red goblet lay. 'Now we have our date. You know what it is?'

'Yes,' said the three women in unison. 'Arretine ware.'

Epilogue

'Teeth,' said Gerry looking up at the screen and then out into the audience. Her mouth was dry. 'Teeth,' she said again and there was a titter from someone sitting in the back row. She looked back at the screen and swallowed hard. She would not let her nerves get the better of her. Sue had trusted her to present their results, and she would show she was worthy of that trust.

She had worked hard over the six months. Now, she understood how lead was absorbed by tooth enamel throughout childhood and every region had different proportions of the four variants of lead – the isotopes – so you could tell where a person grew up just from analysing their teeth. Sue had let her use the skeletons she had excavated herself and she had some really exciting results she wanted to share.

It was a pity Peter wasn't here. He had been surprisingly keen to keep on seeing her at first but had lost interest as her work absorbed her. He had now met someone else and she had heard through the grapevine that he would soon be married. It didn't worry her one bit. She now had the funding she needed to go on to do a PhD thanks to the paper she had written on variation in lead isotope using content of tooth enamel from skeletons in East Anglia. She only wanted him there because he would appreciate the irony of her findings after the joke he made about him being of Roman descent and her Icenian ancestry.

She looked again into the audience and caught Sue's eye. She took a deep breath and read out the title of the slide, 'The importance of lead isotope variation in tooth enamel in identifying the place of origin.' Her voice was firm and authoritative. Her confidence increased. 'That sounds incredibly dull,' she said, 'but let me tell you a story. 'Once upon a time, there was a beautiful Icenian woman and a handsome Roman soldier. Whilst their worlds were collapsing around them, their people were fighting each other, war was raging and death and destruction were everywhere, they met and fell in love and lived happily ever after.'